The Sanskari Rebel and other stories

by

Swati Verma

Noel Lorenz House of Fiction

Title of Book: The Sanskari Rebel and other stories

Author: Swati Verma

First Published in Bharat in March 2025 by Noel Lorenz House of Fiction

ISBN 13: 978-93-48543-74-5

Published & Printed by

Noel Lorenz House of Fiction

Headquarters - Kolkata, West Bengal, Bharat

154A, KCG Road, Kolkata - 700050

www.noellorenz.com

"You cannot cross the sea merely by standing and staring at the water."

~.Rabindranath Thakur.~

Contents

About the Book

------ ^ ------

This book "The Sanskari Rebel and other stories" is a collection of 12 short stories that delve into the minds and thoughts of various characters in unique situations. Each story captures the little emotions, the uncensored thoughts, and ends with a certain realization. The stories are relatable to younger as well as older generations. Belonging to different genres, each story touches upon various human emotions and reactions. While some end with a sense of loss, others bring out hope. Every negative emotion like judgement, exploitation, embarrassment, social differences, lack of compassion and gender bias are overcome with realizations, righteousness, acceptance, love and compassion.

The author of this book has picked these stories from her observation of people around her, since she was a child. And she strongly believes in the interesting turn of events as depicted in her stories, that feels like magic, but can happen to anyone with good intentions. Good always attracts the good, this is the law of the universe.

Swati Verma

------ ^ ------

Author

About the Author

------ ^ ------

Writer at heart, creative by experience and engineer by education - a perfect mix! This is Swati Verma and her journey described in one sentence. The variety of roles she has lived through, seeps into her writing, enriching it!

Though she hails from the beautiful hills of Kerala, higher education and work made her move away from this heavenly abode. Having moved across the country, she found her second home in the city of dreams, Mumbai, where she found the wings to express her thoughts and discovered her passion for writing. She worked as a creative and scriptwriter for television shows and short films.

As an Author, she found her footing in Anthologies 'Fall to Pieces', a book about breaking stereotypes, 'Aranyani', another book poetically expressing the bond between women and nature, and 'Soulful Stardust - in the quest of light', another poetic collection that landscapes through human emotions, experience and imagination. Her solo book titled "Had I Not Lost Myself" released on Amazon that speaks about Teenage Rebellion and their Identity Crisis. Another recent addition to her collection of stories is 'Ripples II' where she has written about a journey of a true alchemist in the age of social media.

Chapter 1

Robin-In-The-Hood

Under a moon-lit sky, there is an empty park that buzzes with the sounds of night insects, disrupting the calmness of the silent night. Leaves rustle as a gentle breeze passes through. In the dark corners of the park, I sit, all alone. I feel distressed seeing this paper in my hand. I don't want to cry, I finally have a plan. But these tears, they don't stop. They never listen. The roads are empty and on the other side, I see this big bungalow dimly lit in the darkness of the night. I breathe in I breathe out, telling myself I need to do this. I have watched this bungalow for some time now and I am well-prepared. I look at my watch and its 2 AM, time to put plan into Action! I fold the paper and put it in my pocket. I do a little spot running, energizing and warming up, while mumbling my prayers. I cross the road, walking towards the bungalow. Suddenly one of the guards has woken up and gets up from his seat to stretch his body. I duck to hide behind the boundary wall eyeing the guard from its corner. The guard drinks some water, adjusts his chair and slouches on it in a semi lying down position. I know how useless these guards are. I have watched them through the night, sleeping away to glory, while I have been busy snooping around finding my way into this bungalow.

I tiptoe sticking close to the boundary wall to reach the other side that has a small gate in the backyard. There is a big bush on its right side. I pull out a green bag hidden in its greenery. I had planted it last night near this very small gate in the backyard and what can hide green better than green itself. I climb the railing as silently as possible and jump into the premises. I land gently on the cushiony grass in their lawn and sprint across to reach a place from where the balcony is clearly visible. Taking out a rope from the bag, I aim it to hook on to the railing. Damn! I missed it! I try again and Hooray!! The anchor clings on to the railing strongly. I check the link once and then start to climb up, my view fixed towards the front yard for any sign of security guards. I was definitely not in their line of sight!

As I inch closer, my pace fastens. I hold on to the railing and pull myself up. Seeing a pair of slippers in the balcony, I check the other side by stretching my neck high up and swiftly down. Phew! It's clear, just an abandoned pair of slippers. I cross over to the other side colliding into the swing. It makes a screeching noise but I hold it still to make the noise stop immediately. Through the window, I can see two people tucked into their warm blankets. I check if they have moved or woken up because of the noise. Slowly and steadily, I move towards the door after crossing the windows. Through the glass of the window pane, in that dimly lit room, someone under the blanket moves. I hold my breath still and stop moving. False Alarm! That someone just turned to the other side. I unlock the door and it opens easily, though with a little noise. I check again but all is quiet. Just the snoring sounds fill the room. Thankfully the door wasn't locked otherwise it would be extra work for me. I close the door with minimum noise.

The room speaks of class and richness, exquisite furniture and huge flat screen TV and unique antique pieces collected from all over the world. The whole room is very well decorated. I scan the room noiselessly till I reach another door across the room and open it slowly. There is a long empty corridor as I peep out. The coast is clear! Seeing no one in sight, I make a quick exit from the bedroom and tip toe over the carpeted floors scanning everything around. Moving steadily and carefully till I reach another door a few meters away. Ah Finally!! This is the room! I slowly turn the door knob and a slight creak sound makes me stop. It's a dark room, unlike the rest of the house which had some light.

Suddenly I hear a wheel chair moving, its metallic sound getting louder. I think it's coming towards me! I jump into the dark room and shut the door. Its pitch dark but the moonlight is streaming into the room. My eyes take a few seconds to adjust and now the room is partially visible to me. My eyes first fall on the big rocking chair on the other side of the room. This is where I am supposed to be! I hear the wheel chair sound right outside the room and I just slide under the bed. A pair of feet walks in with a wheelchair with another pair of feet on it. They stop near the bed. A lady's voice is heard saying, "Don't forget to give me the keys. I will take the things from the trunk and keep it in the locker. It's not safe to keep so much at home." She switches on the light while speaking. Voice of an old lady is heard saying, "I am tired, let me sleep now!" The other lady, I think is putting this old lady to bed while she continues to speak, "you very well know how much Aviral needs that money for growing our business, after all its for our family only right?" Old lady says, "I understand, goodnight beta." The lady sighs,

"Goodnight Maa." And I see her walking out of the room and switching the lights off again, into pitch darkness. My eyes need to adjust again. I turn towards the other side, the window, the moonlight streaming in. It's all so poetic. I hear the old lady murmuring to herself, "I very well know about all your needs, may Krishna bless you all!" This old lady, she is still awake. I have to wait here till she drifts off to deep sleep. As my eyes have readjusted again, I turn back and I see a handkerchief on the floor, very close to the bed. I grab it and it makes a clinking noise. Aha the keys! I turn to the other side again. Near the foot of the rocking chair, there is a small trunk. By now, the room is filled with the snoring sound of the old lady. So finally, it's time to move! I slither across the floor towards the rocking chair. As I reach the trunk at the foot of the rocking chair, I use the key tied to the handkerchief to unlock it. The lock is a little old and rusty. With great difficulty and strength, I finally manage to open it.

Suddenly, there is some movement. Oops the snoring has stopped! I was so engrossed in opening the trunk that I did not realize that. There is a sound of moaning and the bed creaking. The old lady is up! I hold my breath and lay still; only no movement in this darkness can save me as I am no more under the bed, but lying on the floor, completely exposed. I hear her pick up a glass and drink water. She keeps the glass down and lies back down as the bed creaks. I am just praying that she drifts off to sleep soon. I don't have much time left!

Thankfully, she falls asleep within a few seconds. Her soft snoring confirms that. I raise my hand slowly to lift the lid of the trunk as soundlessly as possible. I put my hand in and pull out the red bag. I immediately put it in my green bag. My hand goes in again fishing for some cash and here it is. I pull out a few bundles of money and place it in my bag. The bag is zipped up and then I lower the lid of the trunk and close it. Though it makes a little sound, the old lady sleeps soundly.

After I lock the trunk, I slither back under the bed. I leave the key with the handkerchief exactly where it was lying before. I get up slowly and noiselessly and reach the door. As I open the door partially, the dim lighting outside seeps into the room. I turn back to see the room. It is so simple, a complete contrast to the other room. Just a bed, a trunk, a rocking chair and this old lady on the bed, covered in blanket, deep in sleep, but wrinkles on her forehead so deep. There is no sign of happiness in her life, poor thing. Maybe now she will get her freedom.

Suddenly my watch vibrates. Oh No! Just five more minutes to go! I close the door and retrace my footsteps. I tiptoe back through the same corridor and reach the other door. I slowly open it with a little creaking sound, which thankfully drowns under the snoring sounds of the people sleeping on the bed. Carefully traversing through the room, I reach to the balcony door. Just then I hear a thud. Something has fallen to the floor. Damn! One of the two people might have woken up hearing this loud sound. I turn around hoping I have not been seen yet when I see a woman directly looking at me. She starts yelling, "Thief!!Thief!!" I rush across the room immediately and exit it, before she either wakes her partner up or gets up from the bed herself!

Breathing heavily, I reach the stairs and drop down my bag first. Then I rush down the stairs and stop only once I reach the ground floor. I can hear footsteps and commotion. I think the lady has called the guards too. I look up to check, they haven't even reached the stairs.I pick my bag and enter a dark hallway straining to see the way ahead. I find a small store room and go hide behind the cupboard in between a lot of junk. Lights are being switched on as a man descends the stairs with loud thud sounds of his rubber slippers. The lady is shouting from upstairs asking if he found someone and he responds in a no! There are lot of footsteps heard rushing here and there. I just hold my breath and sit still. As I hear the footsteps moving away and getting feeble in a few minutes, I slide up the glass window on the opposite side of the cupboard and I can see the back gate from there. I jump out, imbalanced, falling on my head first, with my bag almost hitting me. I gain my composure and slowly stand up straight taking a deep breath. I hear some commotion at the front gate. So, the lazy guards are finally up! I just move swiftly wasting no more time till I reach the big bushy plant and the small gate next to it.

I have successfully jumped out and now all I know is I have to reach the bench in the garden across the road in the next two minutes. I cross the road from afar so that I am nowhere close to the boundary wall of the bungalow. Once I have crossed the road, I shed the black jacket and in my plain white t-shirt and black jeans with a green bag across my shoulder, I pretend to walk like any normal person on the road. I walk fast and enter the garden premises. I leave my green bag near the lonely bench where I was seated earlier and turn towards the road. I rush out and see a taxi parked on the roadside. I go into the boot of the car and close it partially allowing me some air and the view of this moonlit street.

Another car pulls in just then. A man comes out of the garden with the same green bag and hands it over to another man who just got out of the car. The former is wearing tattered muddy clothes and his hands are shivering in fear and nervousness. But as soon as he sees this little girl in her pink frock running towards him, shouting papa, his face lights up! She jumps into his arms and I see him in tears as he hugs her daughter. He is not shivering anymore. He just holds on to her for a while, while the other car drives away.

The man carries his daughter in his arms and safely puts her in the taxi. I immediately exit the boot of the car and hide behind the bushes. The man sits in the driver's seat and tells his daughter that he will drop her home, only then take on another ride. Today he will be on night duty. Daughter complains a little but they are happy and they drive away. I watch all this and feel so relieved and a smile spread on my face. I look on the other side and there is still commotion in the bungalow and its premises are being searched. I can't stop smiling. I look up and the old lady is standing near her rocking chair, at the moonlit window. She is looking at me directly. In the partial light of the moon falling on her face, I could see that she was smiling too!

I had never met her until a month back in this very park when I had just moved into this neighbourhood and loved going for my morning walks to the park. She was often seen at the park walking slowly with her cane along with a middle-aged man who looked like her caretaker. We exchanged smiles often. One day, she lost her glasses somewhere in the park. I helped her find it and we started talking. She told me she lived in the bungalow right across the street and I told her how fortunate she is to live in such a mansion. I remember her words vividly even today "Son, I'd rather stay in a wooden cottage than this glass mansion. It is that fragile!" I corrected her saying it's a concrete building and she laughed so hard. Only later I understood what she meant.

One morning, I was sprinting through the park when I saw her sitting on a bench, wiping tears off her eyes. I joined her and on insistence, she told me it was her caretaker whose daughter is kidnapped. "I have all the wealth but I don't have the liberty to give it to anyone. My daughter and Son-in-law won't allow me. I really want to help him son! I fought with my daughter but she thinks he is lying to get money from us, when I know that's not true." I feel bad for her. The wealth that is lawfully hers, she should have the freedom to decide what she wants to do with it. Children cannot demand like this, they should respect their parents' decision and honour their wishes. The old lady was inconsolable and I told her to give me one round around the park to come up with a solution. As I reached back to her, I knew what needs to be done. I picked a chapter from one of my mystery novels and decided to help her and teach her selfish children, some harsh lesson! She helped me with the blueprint of the house and the way to reach the trunk. But there was no balcony to her room directly, so I had to use the more difficult path. She had the keys to the trunk, so she made sure I find it near the foot of her bed. We had a secret code too, that if she felt there was some danger nearby, she would sit up on her bed and I should pause right at that moment till she drifts back to sleep or at least pretends to drift back to sleep. I don't think she could sleep through all this. That is how much it meant to her!

And that is how we planned everything and finally helped the caretaker. I had put on the cloak of Robin Hood that night and put my martial art skills to use. I felt the real worth of acquiring those skills that night when I could bring a smile on her distressed face. Even if I had to rob, dirty my hands, my soul felt cleansed with the blessings of this old lady that will stay with me forever!

"Karma is less in your action, more in your intention!"

Chapter 2

Phobias of the Mind

In a dimly lit room, someone is panting vigorously. A hand is shivering and struggling to reach the office-desk bell. It's a girl's hand and she hits a few things that drop on the floor. A glass of water shatters and water spills on the floor, spreading everywhere. Her long tresses fall on her face and she pulls them to one side. Frail and pale, this girl is freaking out completely. She is holding her heart as it races, almost feeling like her chest would explode. Her hand is still jostling through the table until it finally gets to a small office-desk bell. It rings loudly on being pressed. Just then a loud clang is heard. It's the pendulum clock and it echoes in her ears. She shuts her ears and runs here and there erratically, colliding into a few things. She is literally getting a panic attack. Suddenly the clock stops. She stops struggling too. She turns around and sees her reflection in the water on the floor. She starts yelling, "no! no!" and turns to the other side, losing her nerve again. Quickly something moves towards her from behind and she screams. Everything goes dark.

"Wake up beta! Chhaya, please beta, wake up!" I open my eyes slowly and hearing my mother's voice, her gaze, it's so comforting, it's familiar, I really needed it right now. I am in her arms, I just move closer to her to feel more secure. I turn to look at the glass window with fear in my eyes. The image of that reflection still looms in my mind. My mother follows my gaze and she immediately rushes and shuts the drapes covering the glass window completely. Now I can breathe!

In another two hours, we leave home. My mother is driving the car while I occupy the adjacent seat. It feels good to smell the flowers, watch the greenery, feel the warmth of the sun and a soft breeze brushes my face as the car drives through the small lanes. My mother tells me to close the window but I don't want to! Feeling all this has become a rare thing for me now and I don't want to waste a single opportunity to miss it. It's like take it when you can, as much as you can. In captivity, these memories are what keep me going.

As we reach the main road, the car speeds up. The wind blows through my hair, messing up my long tresses. My mother parks the car to one side of the road. "This is ridiculous!" My mother says this while checking herself out in the side mirror, "Look at your state!" she turns towards me and starts adjusting my hair, "we are going to a party and you have messed up your hair like this!" She dabs my face with a tissue, "you are a grown up now! Be a little conscious about your looks, at least before a party!!" She turns to take out the wrapped gift from the back seat once she is done straightening me out, "Now we are going to Tanya's birthday, so behave properly! Don't embarrass me!!" I just exit the car and bang the door in anger. My mother stares at me in anger, then shakes her head and follows me into a big beautiful brick house.

As soon as we enter the room, a group of ladies come to greet us. I just fold my hands in Namaste and give a feeble smile to everyone. I want to just move away and I am waiting for that perfect opportunity. Just then Tanya joins the group and meets my mother warmly. My mother hands over the gift to her and hugs her saying, "you are looking so pretty beta!" Tanya thanks her and then turns towards me. She asks me how I am and I just ignore her and leave this chatty group. I walk across the hall and find a corner where only a group of kids are playing and it's fun to watch their activities. They are all bundled together in a circle and I peep in to see what they are playing. Its spin the bottle! I just stiffen and I start feeling breathless again as I see the bottle spinning continuously.

The bottle starts to slow down gradually and I just keep eyeing the bottle and then it stops. I look up and it's pointing at a young timid boy. All kids start chanting "Aarav! Aarav! Aarav!" but he says truth and everyone groans! Tanya is sitting next to me and she says, "I had thought of such a nice dare for him, truth is so boringgg!!" I look at him, my younger brother Aarav who is not so social and mostly I am the only one he likes to talk or listen to. I tell him to change his decision. He is hesitant but relents just because I insisted.

With a wicked smile on her face, Tanya jumps up from her seat spelling out the dare, "As the clock strikes 12, he has to stand in front of the mirror and say Bloody Mary three times." She looks at all our puzzled faces and continues, "you know what happens when you do that..." she takes a pregnant pause and everyone looks at her without blinking. She is enjoying this and acts it out while saying, "A hand comes out of the mirror and kills you!!" Aarav gets really scared hearing this. I shut her up, "What rubbish! No such thing will happen! Don't scare everyone for no reason!" Tanya doesn't stop there. She looks at Aarav and says, "There are spirits captured in the mirror, watching us! They cannot come out during the day, only at night they become active!"Aarav looks at the clock and only a few minutes left to 12 midnight. He looks at me, really terrified. I realize what Tanya is doing. She is trying to scare Aarav so that he fails to do the dare and then her team can win. I tell my brother to not believe her, "She is bluffing my brother. She wants us to lose. Trust me! We need this point to win. Come on Aarav, you can do this!" Tanya laughs and says it's not a lie, people have died doing this. I ask her to prove it and we get into a verbal fight. Aarav stops us and says he will do it for his team. It's already two minutes to 12! Aarav goes into the bedroom and stands in front of the mirror. We all are standing outside, watching him. He turns back and looks at me with rheumy eyes. I tell him, "Come on Aarav, you are so strong!! My superman brother! Let's defeat them." Just then the clock strikes 12 and it will now clang 12 times. At the first clang, all the kids move away from that room. Everyone is a little scared. Tanya wants to win the game badly, so she tries one last thing. She switches off the light of the room and runs out closing the door behind her.

I was tying my shoe lace when I heard my brother scream. That is when I realized the door to the room is locked. I rush towards it to open the door and Tanya pushes me away. I fall flat on the floor and bruise my knees and elbows. The clock continues to strike and at the 12th strike, I somehow get up again and stare angrily at Tanya. Though I was really angry at Tanya and wanted to hit her back, I was more worried about my brother Aarav. So, I rush to open the door first. It was all quiet inside and the room was pitch dark. My fingers scramble on the wall to locate the switch board. As I switch on the lights, I see my brother sprawled on the floor, covered in blood. I scream my heart out in shock and pain.

I feel a hand on my shoulders and I jump. My heart is racing and I am perspiring. I turn around to see it's my mother. She looks worried, "are you ok Chhaya?" I nod my head silently. She rubs the sweat off my forehead, "honey we need to leave soon, go have some food." I walk towards the salad counter while my mother is busy on some other counter serving some biryani. As I pick a plate, the tissue slips from my hand and falls down. I bend to pick it up and the rotating fan mounted on the wall blows it away in another direction. I try to catch it and end up near the adjacent wall. As I pick the tissue and I am about to leave, my eyes fall on the wall on my right and there is a huge mirror mounted on the wall. I freeze on the spot!

Suddenly the whole room goes dark and I am alone in the room holding the torch to my face. This is the same room where my brother died that day. I stand in front of that same mirror and as the clock clangs 12 times at midnight, I say Bloody Mary three times and then I request her to give me back my brother. I ask for Aarav with my eyes closed, terrified of getting killed or seeing the ghost in the mirror. I open my eyes a little as there is complete silence and no movement in the mirror. Just then something moves behind me and I turn to check. There is nothing! Getting more scared, I close my eyes again and beg Bloody Mary for my brother. I keep muttering my prayers and requests in a single breath. As silence looms over again, I build the courage to open my eyes again. As I open my eyes, I see a disfigured reflection looking back at me. It's looking at me continuously. I start to pant and perspire. I scream and the plate in my hand falls to the floor and crashes. Everyone's attention is drawn towards me. Please stop looking at me all of you, all your peering eyes. My mother and two or three of our relatives come and help her take me to a sofa nearby. They make me sit and offer me water. Tanya is standing right in front of me, looking uncomfortable. I look at her, pulling my clothes away, just feeling very suffocated. I want to go out. I tell my mother I want to step out. But as I get up in a rush to leave, everything blacks out!

I hear my mother's voice in the background as she is ranting about how that night after Aarav's death, my life changed forever. I open my eyes and I am lying on a bed, it's a clinic! I see a man talking to my mother from across the table and making notes. Tanya is sitting next to my mother, looking concerned. My mother continues to complain how I have made her life so difficult, "Now we cannot even take her to a public place because as soon as she spots any mirror and sees her reflection on any surface, she starts freaking out!" I look away, tears in my eyes. I remember my little brother Aarav every day of my life and feel guilty that I convinced him for that dare. How does someone ever come out of that guilt? Every time I see Tanya, that guilt only amplifies!

Doctor comes up to me and sensing that, I quickly wipe my tears. He looks at me, "Hello Chhaya, finally you are up. I am Dr. Anand Sahay and I am here to listen to you. He offers me his hand and I get up taking his support. I sit next to my mother as the doctor asks my mother, "Why didn't you take her to a doctor earlier? You allowed her condition to get from bad to worse!" Mother justifies her actions, "Me and my husband, we always felt she would get better with age, that all this were just childish fears!"

Doctor straightens up, "It's because of your negligence that she is in this state today. Rather than being embarrassed, you should have been her strongest support. If you had accepted and believed in her condition, it wouldn't have got worse. Now she is ailing from a chronic case of Spectrophobia, a fear of reflections. Whenever there is a mirror in front of her, she would see a disfigured reflection like it's her childhood monster Bloody Mary who took her brother away. Am I right Chhaya?" I am appalled by how much he could understand me in just a few minutes. I don't think anyone could understand my problem this well till date. I have tears in my eyes as I nod in a yes. He holds my hand, "See I know your difficulty because I have seen my sister face it too. How childhood incident can scar your mind so badly that you see what you imagine happened to your brother that day. Tanya's story has become your truth because you did not believe her story but that is what killed your brother, just like she was saying that day." Mother exclaims, "Yes that's why she doesn't even talk to Tanya properly. Poor girl has apologized a million times." Doctor stops her, "I would request you to let me talk to Chhaya alone for some time. I want to hear her story. Tanya can stay and listen if she wants, but nobody interrupts. Please understand this is very important." From that day onwards, my mother never interfered. And she never made me feel that I embarrassed her. She never forced me to any social events, waiting patiently for me to get better. Dr. Anand Sahay has become my best friend and it's so easy to talk to him. I have seen even Tanya burst into tears while talking to him. She has also lived with the guilt and I don't hate her anymore, like I used to.

It's been almost six months of Hypnotherapy sessions now. I could feel something change within me with every session. I cried out all the guilt I felt and kept healing from that. My mother has also changed her ways after multiple sessions with the doc. She feels responsible for me and makes sure I have a healthy environment at home. She and I would have emotional talks now, about Aarav, how she was grieving her son too. It feels good to have heart to heart conversation with my mother. My father is mostly away due to work, but when he comes home, he gives me all his attention and takes me out for nature walks. I try to see my reflection on the surface of the water. Mostly, nothing else is there, no disfigured face, only my reflection, but I still feel it will come to me from somewhere and even that thought scares me. Every day is a battle but thanks to my doc, I now know how to.

Aarav's real story I know now, how he hit his head in the mirror when he panicked in the dark. There was no Bloody Mary. Listening to this everyday even during hypnotherapy, kind of planted this thought permanently in my head. The root of negative thoughts kept getting uprooted in bits and pieces helping me progress positively.

But today I again feel the nervousness and anxiety. Doc wants to see me and we would try looking into the mirror and he promises to stand with me. My hands are shivering and I am feeling woozy in my head. I stand there in front of the mirror, clutching doc's hand tightly. He is smiling and it's just the two of us in the mirror. Good so far! But that changes as he starts moving out of frame, still holding my hands but his reflection disappears. It is just me now! I get that feeling again that something will come now from some unknown direction. I clutch tightly to doc's hand. He reminds me to breathe deeply and asks me to see my beautiful dress. Sometimes with beautiful dresses, with props, something different that catches my attention and distracts me from that looming thought, he tries to normalize looking into the mirror for me. And every time I can stand longer in front of the mirror.

It has been three long years now. I go to school like everyone. After assembly, when I go to washroom to wash my hands, there is a mirror at the wash basin. I see myself and adjust my tie which is a little loose. I hear footsteps coming towards me and I continue to look into the mirror. I know it's nothing. There has never been any Bloody Mary and there never will be. No one is coming towards me, except my friends who join me there. I take a deep breath and we chat happily. Tanya is also in the same school, though not in my group of friends. But we talk to each other now and meet at family functions. Randomly, one of my friends point out in mid-conversation, how much she loves my blue headband. I turn and check it out in the mirror and smile. World is good again and so am I. I have finally healed!

"Acknowledgement of a trauma is the first step to healing!"

Chapter 3

Out of the Box

A long corridor from my office to the gate and everyone has left for home. Damn this presentation! I had to stay late to complete it. And still, I could not. Now I will have to go home and finish it. Say goodbye to any sleep tonight. But that is not the only thing that is worrisome. The fact that I will have to travel back home for almost three hours in a shared cab with two or three strangers this late at night is more unnerving. Once I am done booking a cab on Ola, and made it to the pick-up point, I could see that the cab is still about 5 minutes away. One or two autos pass by, and interestingly when you don't need them, they stop for you. And on top of that, seeing a girl standing alone on a lonely street makes her very vulnerable in the eyes of men either with the intention of protecting her or ogling and teasing her for their pleasure.

You see, I have already placed these men in two boxes. I have already formed an opinion based on what to expect, but if I hadn't, I would be very naïve and careless. So even if we do not want to, we end up putting people in boxes and it is so spontaneous that it cannot be controlled.

My thoughts get interrupted by a vehicle fast approaching me. The cab stops right in front of me and I check the number plate and compare the information given on my phone. I ask for the driver's ID. It's a she, her name is Sheela. Thank God for female cab drivers now-a-days. Somehow, it's a little comforting. I get into the cab, all women in it. Front seat is already taken much to my dismay. I am stuck with two ladies, squeezing myself into the backseat. The lady in the middle is very bulky while the other one has a medium built like me. Thus, we both are sitting pressed hard against the doors of the cab, while the lady in the middle has taken like 50% of the seating space. Quite an uncomfortable ride!

My mind immediately gets to work, observing all the ladies in the cab and forming an opinion about them. Accordingly, I start placing them in boxes of judgements. And my first target becomes the fat lady sitting next to me! I wonder how people can be so callous about their health to bloat so much. I am very health conscious, and since I tend to put-on weight easily, I work out regularly to burn my calories and maintain myself. Discipline is the order of my life and I wake up early to be able to make time for all this. I am sure she must be lazy and a foodie as well or could she be a mother?! Still, that's no excuse to remain like this. My elder sister is a mother of two and she is so fit and fine.

Just then cab takes a sudden right and Oh God! She is completely leaning on me. I straighten myself and she too moves back to her original position. The girl on the other side looks at my plight and gives me a smile. I smile back, I am sure she must be thinking what I am thinking.

This sudden turning happens again and again she is on me. The other girl tells the driver Sheela "didi, pull over to one side, I will sit in the middle so that everyone can be more comfortable." The fat lady thanks the other girl as the cab parks itself and they swap places. Uff! I am so relieved. Though at the same time, something inside me just squirmed. Instead of judging this fat lady, why didn't I think of this solution?

I look at the girl sitting next to me and I feel so small, like I am a very petty person. The fat lady suddenly speaks up "I am sorry you guys were so uncomfortable because of me. By the way I am

Sidra, and you? The girl next to me says "I am Rashmi and please don't apologise, already there is so less space in the car. This car is definitely not for five people." And she laughs. But Sidra says, "it's not just that. I am taking so much space as I am the fat one."

Feeling sorry for her, I interrupt "Its ok dear, some people tend to put-on quite easily, like I do. But I work hard at the gym to stay fit." I have always been very upfront about how I feel and my job in advertising has only heightened my bluntness. An awkward silence followed by uncomfortable smiles, as she says sheepishly "I am suffering from thyroid and that is why I have put-on so much in last six months. I am on medication and I am hoping I can be my thin self again."

Oh wow! This poor thing! I think I have been very harsh, and I don't know how I could take it back. That is why they say think before you speak because words that come out, cannot be taken back. As a sudden reflex and a surge of guilt that I needed to cover up, I apologize immediately and try to empathize with her. Here comes the diplomacy! How did I become like this; I wonder? I always find people who are very upfront and open about their shortcomings like this girl Sidra, very courageous. I mean I could never talk about my health problems openly like this.

The cab brakes and brings me out of my thoughts. The lady sitting in the front seat is telling about her problem, something about her liver, but I could not understand anything from the middle of the conversation. They kept talking throughout our drive to Sidra's place. Hers was the first stop. Ahh, I really do enjoy my space. And can you blame me? After spending all day in a small cubicle, in front of the laptop, anyone would crave for space and freedom. Now it was just me and the other girl Rashmi in the backseat. We exchanged smiles. She seems like a very content girl, happy with her life. I think only people who are happy from within can care and think about others. Just then, the lady sitting in the front seat asks me if I am married and I tell her that I am not. She starts asking about me, just random things about my life. I hate it when someone does that. I am a very private person and I don't like it when people do that. I try to keep my answers as short as I could.

Just then Rashmi's phone rings. Her ringtone is some tacky 90s Bollywood romantic song. She picks up and unfortunately, due to the voice leaking problems on phones these days, I can hear the other side too. It's a guy speaking in a very harsh tone and he is yelling at her for being this late. He warns her to quit her job or things could get really difficult. Poor thing, all she keeps mumbling is "I am not alone. Can we do this when I reach home?" I think the guy is drunk and he continues to ramble some shit. Rashmi cuts the phone as she just notices that I am staring in her direction. I got so engrossed in their fight that I didn't realize I was violating her privacy. Oh shoot! I am sorry! I apologize immediately as she looks at me uncomfortably. She gives me a feeble smile and looks away, outside. Not sure but I could feel she is hiding a tear or two.

Yet another nice woman having a horrible life after marriage. If a guy marries a wife who earns, why doesn't he give her the same rights that he has. After all she is not dependent on him for anything and I am sure she can take care of herself too. It's the men who can't. Only if their big fat egos could accept that ever! This is precisely the reason why I am commitment phobic. I think I can never deal with this injustice. I hear sobs and I look towards my side. Rashmi is sniffing and controlling herself. I really don't know what to say to her to make her feel better. Sheela, our driver speaks up "don't shed tears madam! This happens to every one of us. Now my husband is suffering from paralysis, so I must work to earn money for my children so

I can educate them, but even he was the same when he was fine. He never let me work and would hit me if I even spoke to someone. But God has his own way of doing justice. Not that I am happy for his condition, but my years of tears and curses might have inflicted this on him. And today he is so helpless that seeing me standing on my own feet is his biggest punishment.

Wow! She is already my hero. Some professions and the people working in them might look small in the worldly sense, but they are heroes in their own battles. I mean, to me she is already leading a successful life, even if the definition of success might be different for the world. After all what's more satisfying and fulfilling than living your life on your own terms.

The lady sitting next to the driver, the inquiry queen, who has been questioning every one of us throughout our cab ride, out of nowhere begins to talk about her daughter-in-law and how her son treats her nicely, "So, there are good men in this world too and women like my daughter-in-law who take advantage of that." She goes on with her weird concept that good men always get bad girls and vice-versa. I just sit there wondering why it is relevant to mention it in this situation. I want to say something to shut her up, when Rashmi cuts in. She tells the lady it would be wrong to make any generalizations. And no one in this entire world is all good or all bad. Even my husband has some good qualities as I am sure does your daughter-in-law. The lady mumbles something and goes quiet. She did not receive the kind of reaction she was expecting. I am really beginning to admire this woman Rashmi. There is something about her that makes her so empowered. Even in her grief and distress, she can see the good and gets no satisfaction in pulling other women or men down to justify her stand. I thought I was a feminist but seeing her, I realise what real feminism is. A simple lady, an ordinary woman, but such extraordinary thoughts, such high thinking! Highly admirable!

She has already entered in the good box just like Sheela. Even more than Sheela because I think she must be well educated to be this open and broad-minded. Suddenly, the cab comes to a halt and the lady in the front seat gets down. She wishes us good night and leaves. We drive off and it's just the three of us. Rashmi would be getting off next and I would be the last one. I ask her what she does for a living. She tells me she is a nanny. She adds to it how she got late today as the parents of the child she was looking after, came back very late from the party. They had only booked this cab for her so that she could reach home safe. She had informed her husband too, but once he is drunk, he loses his sense of understanding anything. I ask her what he does. She tells me he works on contractual basis and gets paid sometimes. So, it's not enough to support their household. Out of curiosity, I just blurt out that being a nanny also would not bring enough income. I immediately apologize realizing that I am being too intrusive. But she quietly replies, "Unfortunately parents didn't educate me enough and got me married off early."

I am really surprised to know that a woman less educated can talk so intelligently and has such a good understanding of things. Even my master degree could have never taught me what this girl could teach me in one cab ride. Here I am, with two lesser qualified women, handling marriages, children, abusive husbands and still living on high ideals and setting examples for women in our society like a pro. Life has been a bigger teacher for them than books. That day, I could not put them in any of my pre-conceived boxes as they defied all norms. Their existence made me question my whole belief system and my idea of feminism. And my idea of who belongs to which box based on their first impressions.

I reach home with my head filled with these thoughts. I start retracing back to every man or woman that I have ever placed in boxes based on my notion of them. No two people are all alike but different because of the journey they have been through. All the defined boxes in my mind begin to blur and I could truly understand how everyone has something that makes them "Out of the Box".

"Generalizations limit our experiences and perceptions of others."

Chapter 4

The Changing Definitions of Success

Sitting with 20 other people in a meeting, a meeting about some boring HR program that the HR team of our company have come up with to make our experience at work more interesting, my mind kept wandering with random thoughts while I watched a bus full of company employees walk towards our building through the glass walls. Wow! That's a lot of people streaming in, working in one of the biggest multi-national companies and I am just one of them. When I had joined here, I had such big dreams, was highly ambitious and I took my work too seriously. But it took only two years for me to realize no matter what I do, I am replaceable, unlike my family where I am important, and this realization changed my priorities drastically. I started treating my job like just a job that gives me money to pay my bills. I valued my financial independence even if it came at the cost of being trapped in the golden cages that are these big beautiful buildings with glass walls.

Everyone starts clapping and I join in. I see my boss looking in my direction and calling out my name. He introduces me to the HR and tells her to co-ordinate with me further on this. Why the hell did he choose me now! I don't even have a clue about this as I was hardly listening. Anyways I nod in silence. I exchange numbers with the HR Kriti as I exit the conference room and we decide to meet in the cafeteria for an hour daily to work on this new venture. I was already dreading this added responsibility, unaware that by the end of this, I would have learned a valuable lesson for life!

As I walk back to my workstation, I get a coffee from the coffee machine. I see a few teammates who are already leaving for lunch. I start my task for the day and target to finish at least 40 per cent before lunch. My messenger blinks and I see a message from my friend Mahesh. He adds a few other friends to the chat group, and they start a conversation about where to go for dinner tonight. How do these guys have time to chill? I am mostly busy and being just one seat away from my boss, I am always conscious. I can feel his gaze on me from time to time. Ufff!!

Only if my messenger could stop blinking so profusely!! I see a message from HR Kriti too and she asks if we could meet in one hour to discuss further. I confirm. I let my boss know and decide to go have lunch first. Ohh, I so dread these added responsibilities! I am like the hardworking donkey, who is always burdened with enough work compared to others in my project, then why me again for this? I really don't get my boss sometimes.

As I am about to leave, I receive a mail from my colleague Ankur, regarding the task assigned and the schedule. It is his duty each day to put this mail, but the smart guy that he tries to be, he starts thinking he can assign us tasks like a boss. With time, he became my boss' pet and behaved like a boss when he was not around. I feel some people know how to use any situation to their advantage and this guy is an expert at that. While the others slog their asses to better their skill sets, he entertains our boss and even convinces him that he will be the team's only point of contact for any status updates on tasks that need to reach the boss at the end of each day. So, in a weird way, he was above us, even though he wasn't competent enough technically.

I hated Ankur and I was probably the only one who refused to report to him. I dared to approach my boss always and that would really irritate him. He tried every which way to tame me, even convinced the boss to tell me to report to him instead, but me being me, I just couldn't. So, we were never on best of terms and he always tried to take away the credit for my work and give it to some teammates who did report to him religiously. Office Politics!!

I shut my mail and go to the cafeteria. After a quiet lunch, I meet HR Kriti. I am a little embarrassed, but I still insist that we run through the whole concept once more. So basically, we need to script a small play from our project that talks about how we can improve our work experience. Each project and their teams are supposed to come up with their concept and the best one will get an award. Kriti told me how we can show our day-to-day difficulties at workplace with a tinge of humour for entertainment and show how we can resolve those issues. I like the idea and my mind is already full of the problems that can be portrayed. We decide to meet the next day to discuss things point by point and now get back to our respective work, though I already am a little excited about this initiative by HR department and could already feel my creative juices flowing.

Rest of my day includes completing my tasks with no time to think about the concept of the play. But as soon as I get into my car, my creativity takes the front seat and all the ideas start to rush back. I am sure I don't want to talk about trivial matters and rather talk about the bigger loophole in the corporate system, especially the problem that I face daily. Yes! Ankur would be my main subject because honestly, I don't respect guys like him who thrive on the sole talent of buttering their seniors. Somewhere I wanted to humiliate him in front of the team and discourage such practices.

I am driving faster than usual, but that's ok. I am so excited about something after so long. I feel like I could make a huge difference in the working environment. I reach home and gobble my dinner while exchanging a few pleasantries with my family. I tell them about my new initiative and start making a ppt on the same. Here it goes:

A Naarad muni starts working in their project. His qualification is his talent for gossip and humour...hahahahaha sounds so much like Ankur...I can't wait to execute this plan and give him the taste of his own medicine. I wanted to make it funny and its characters as the characters like Hindu Gods of the heavens. Lord Brahma being the project head, Lord Vishnu being the manager and Lord Shiva, the team lead, my boss and the rest of the team like rest of the Gods in Lord Indra's fort like the lord of wind, Sun God etc...Lord Indra would be my good friend Shankar, who acts well and is a very dynamic personality. So now I have the cast, the story would be some interesting incident that happened last month, when Ankur had tried to over-ride me as usual. Of course, here instead of me, it would be Lord Indra getting into trouble because of Naarad muni and how he is taught a lesson by Indra. The Skelton of the story is clear in my head. I just have to flesh it out. I close my eyes and recalled all that happened a month ago.

I had just reached office and checked my mail when I received a mail from Ankur. The mail was regarding tasks assigned for the day. Also, my boss was coming late that day and he had asked him to handle the call with the client. Generally, we all join the call and are there like passive listeners. So Ankur was quite nervous that day and he was on our heads to give him the status to all that our team was handling. I could see that he had no confidence when it came to technical aspects. All he is good at is buttering the bosses. He asked us all to be a part of the call and talk if he instructs us to do so. Once the call started, he registered his presence. Clients rambled among themselves in their foreign accent. I could see the nervousness on his face.

Then one of them started questioning Ankur. He started off fine and I was waiting to see when he would falter. After all, just kissing your boss's ass should not get you all the opportunities when I am much more deserving to be in that position. I found this favouritism so unfair because merit had no say in all this. I believe my work should talk for me, but when your own boss refuses to listen, what do you do? Anyways a sudden nudge by Shankar brought me out of my trance and I realized that now Ankur was stuck and unable to answer the clients. He looked at us for some help. I really didn't want to, but it was for my task. So, I waited enough to see him embarrassed and then I spoke. And as I always knew, I was good at it and could answer everything well. The call ended and we all went back to doing our work. But as soon as my boss reached, Ankur acted like he took care of everything without even mentioning my contribution. Later that day, my boss called everyone in a meeting and handed me a high priority task on being asked by the clients. I looked at Ankur from the corner of my eyes, but he didn't react. I am sure he must be burning from within, but it serves him right for being such a credit stealer. Yes! This was the story I wanted to tell hoping for my boss to see what the truth is and for Ankur to see the error of his ways.

The day before the event, I met Kriti and her HR team to work out a few last moment details. When I got back to my workstation, there was this wave of anxiety among all my team mates. Manager and my boss were having a discussion about our yearly performance reviews, and to my dismay, Ankur was also made a part of those discussions. Goodbye to my track record of high ratings and good yearly bonus. I am not getting any this year, thanks to Ankur! I wish the play had happened a day before, then I could have just told my boss Ankur's truth. But now, he totally has an advantage. He will take all the credit even in front of the manager. I couldn't put myself to work as my mind was clouded with these thoughts. Just then I receive a mail from the client and I was reminded of the high priority task. So, rest of the day, I will have no time to think about this.

I see my boss come back to his seat. I keep looking at his face, trying to read his expressions. Any micro expressions of positivity would do right now. Meanwhile, Mr. Ankur is surrounded by his buttering bees secretly taking updates from him, ensuring they are good to go. How do these people live with themselves?! Anyways back to work now! I decided my best distraction was to immerse myself in this task, otherwise I will go mad. I put my blinders on and started working on my system. Next, I thought about it only when I was in my bed at night. But the satisfaction of seeing the shock and shame on his face that I would get, after seeing my play made me feel good. I will finally have my revenge! Relaxed, I drift off to sleep in no time.

Next day, I couldn't wait for the play to start. I had jitters in my stomach and couldn't eat or do anything much. After dropping a satisfactory mail to my client, I met with Kriti and her HR team and finally the show begins right in the middle of our bay. I keep eyeing Ankur at every punch that was meant for him. But he looks unperturbed, totally unaware that he is the target of my mockery. The image of his shock and shame in my mind is shattered. How is he not reacting?!

Anyways the play got over and I got a 'good effort' from my manager. I knew this is no winning piece. But my defeat is more in Ankur's silence and calmness. Should I say something to him? Just then Ankur walked up to me and asked about the high priority task. I told him the status trying hard to read some irritation on his calm face. He took the status and left. Of course, he got back to his morning ritual of updating the status of the task and reassigning them if necessary. I also give up and just when I am getting back to my tasks, my boss comes and tells me to check my performance review. I immediately open it and couldn't believe my eyes. I got a high rating this year too. That means good yearly bonus, wohoo! My heart jumps in excitement! I turn around and thank my boss. He advises me to thank Ankur because he really stood up for me in front of the manager. And also, for his whole team, he stood for us all. My boss also appreciated me for supporting Ankur with client interactions, "Now I can count on you too for client calls!!"

I am sure if I look in the mirror right now, the expressions of shock and shame that I was searching on Ankur's face all morning, would be visible on my face. I looked at him and as he looked back, my eyes drifted down in shame. How can I look at him now, I have hated this guy, judged him so much, cursed him every day but he supported me and did not put me down even when he had the opportunity. But I have to thank him. So, I somehow built up the courage to walk up to him. But as I look up, he is not there at his workstation. I search around and there he is with my boss, discussing something. He has that friendly smile. Maybe he also got a good performance review. He exits the bay. I rush out too and call him. He stops and looks confused. I go up to him and thank him for taking a stand for me and my work. Ankur pats my back and tells me I deserve it. I never thought I would hear those words from him. He starts reminding me of how I have handled the most number of high priority tasks successfully and my deliverables are also the highest in our team. I am just amazed at how much he knows about everyone's work in our team. And here I thought he had no skills. How could I be so myopic in my thoughts that always thought technical skill is the only skill that is required? His skill is also very important for us and I can't do what he does, nor can anyone else in our team. And I think my boss realizes that. I am sure even my boss doesn't know things about our team as well as Ankur. I feel another pat on my back, "Hey where are you lost?" It's Ankur, I had totally phased out. I apologize and thank him again. He smiles and gives me a word of advice that I really needed to be told, otherwise I would never have realized it and grown in my career. He explains how if I could connect with the team more, work on my human relationships along with the technical skills, I could even think of promotions in the next term. The way he said it, he is so right!!!!

All my school life, it was about getting first rank in class. And I came here with the same goals, to be the best at my job. But my job was not just to do my part well, but to help my team grow with me. Ankur has taught me a very valuable lesson today and I might be a programming genius, but he is a leader in the making. Rather than hating him, I should learn human skills from him and make myself worthy of becoming a leader.

As I walk back to my workstation, I realize that if Ankur had gotten to script that play, we would have won because he would have spoken about the team and how to better things for all of us. And here I was, in my spite, I couldn't look at the bigger picture. Today, his encouragement and selfless words of advice and his team spirit to uplift everyone in the team has itched the humanity in me to grow up and understand real achievements. Today, he has changed my definition of success forever!!!

"A leader is not just someone who does great things, but also the one who guides his team to do great things."

Chapter 5

The Sanskari Rebel

I often stare at the park overlooking my house. I see the kids playing, ladies gossiping, some health-conscious people brisk walking or jogging and particularly a girl playing with her friends every evening around six. She reminds me of my childhood. She is tall and lean just like I used to be. She is seen playing a different sport every day. Guess what!! So did I when I was her age!

I love sports! While some girls were busy grooming themselves for college every morning and few others busy with their household chores, I and a few like me would reach college early to play some sports. Any sports from badminton to table tennis to volleyball and so on, my tall and lean physique and competitive spirit helped me become excellent at it all. Any sport and I would master it within a few days!

But dare I say anything at home to my parents! Except when once in a blue moon, an aunt from our neighbourhood would call me over and we would play badminton for some time. But even that stopped eventually. To hell with the guy who my mother noticed staring at me from his balcony while I was playing, that small window of freedom was also closed for me!

But this girl, it's such a treat to watch her!! She is really good and I get so engrossed watching her that I feel my mind is totally in the game. Only if I had the remote and this game was like a video game where I was one of the players! Same energy and the same adrenaline rush, I just love the feeling! Well, then why can't i go and play with her? It's not the age that is stopping me from doing this. I would have done the same in normal circumstances but now it's a distant possibility because I am pregnant!

Yes! My husband Akshay and I are having a baby. I am in my last trimester and my maternal leave from work has already started. Marriage and motherhood came to my life unexpectedly. But I always gave my 100 % to everything in life. Going with the flow just seemed like a happier way to live!

As I had just finished nibbling on my melon, the bell rang. It's Disha, my neighbour's daughter. She would come every day around this time and

I would tutor her in Sanskrit and math. Those were her weak subjects and since I was quite proficient in them, I offered to help better her grades. It was a good way to keep my mind occupied and connected with education, the phase that I had enjoyed the most!

A happy go-lucky girl, it is difficult for Disha to be completely focused on her studies and she would often enjoy rambling about her day-to-day issues. I have to constantly remind her to finish her studies first. Sometimes I succeed, but today is definitely not one of those days. She had a major fight with her mother regarding her not doing the work given to her. She was supposed to fold her clothes and arrange it in the cupboard, but they were lying sprawled all over her bed like a heap of garbage. She is lazy and she would always convince her parents about some tests that she needs to prepare for and escape doing the household chores. I am glad times have changed and girls have the option to say no to such work. It was very different for us and that is what I try to make her understand so that she values the freedom her parents are giving her, despite her low grades.

Education was very important to me and hard work and intelligence graced me with being a state rank holder in my boards. Despite a joint family that did not believe in a girl's education and tried every day to interrupt my study time with making tea for the relatives or calling for other chores at home, I strived to always be a topper in my class. It was my immense determination and focus that made me religiously wake up every morning before sunrise and revise my lessons while everyone else was sleeping. Those hours were the only undisturbed hours I had!

Despite all this hard work, the promise my father gave me after I excelled in my 10th boards that if I achieve the same accolade in my 12th boards, then I can do my graduation from a very good college in Delhi, was just overlooked and drowned under the scrutiny of my relatives who objected to how my father could send a daughter away to a distant place among strangers for higher studies. Ironically, that same daughter will be married to a stranger but that was acceptable!

That is how the society functions. Everyone kept telling my father what will she do with so much education when ultimately, she has to get married and run a household. As it is, even my studying in a convent school seemed like an unnecessary expenditure to everyone but my saving grace was that I was performing so well that my relatives had no basis to convince my father to stop my education!

Disha is just speechless hearing all this. She tells me how I have made her count her blessings. She regrets fighting with her mom for silly things. I tell her to focus on her studies and do well to make up for all the anger and shouting on her mother. And those words actually work like magic as we complete a whole chapter that day!

The due delivery date of my pregnancy was fast approaching and my mother came to stay with me as it was getting difficult to manage alone. My in-laws also joined us two days before my due date. My hormones were all over the place but everyone was being patient and caring towards me. While we were sitting in the living room, the discussion somehow drifted to how it's common for couples to have only one child these days. Akshay and I were being advised to try for another especially if we end up with a daughter. At least one grandson must be there in the family.

Oh God! Time has flown, but the thought process has not changed a bit! Daughters are supporting their families, multi-tasking by taking care of their families and their jobs well and despite all these capabilities, she can never replace a son in the mind of the parents. I was reminded of my childhood when I was born two years after my elder sister. Everyone was waiting for a son and

I was a total disappointment. My mother was told by everyone to try again for a son and to facilitate their ambitions, I was sent off to my maternal grandparents till I was like eight. They loved me a lot and that is why I was always more attached to them than my parents. After all they held me close at my most tender age.

And this legacy of making me feel unwanted did not end just there. As we grew up, eligible to get married, my sister was married off and within six months, I was also married off to some guy I barely knew. I hadn't even completed my graduation, but my fate was thrown into the hands of a stranger. It was only my sheer good luck that I ended up with Akshay who let me finish my graduation and apply for jobs. And what a lovely coincidence it was, when I got my first job offer from Delhi. If not as a student, as an employee, I earned my way to Delhi. I think somewhere God was guiding me and supporting me because I was not given what I was promised by my parents. Akshay convinced his parents and shifted his job to Delhi too. We started our life together in Delhi and here we are today, about to start our own family.

I hope to break these few norms that our parents believed in but the sanskari me, would never allow me to talk back. I think it's the actions of the rebel in me that will do the talking when the time comes!

"Actions always speak louder than words, so become the change you want to see."

Chapter 6

What if Evolution is more than what meets the eye?

Vast Ocean and a diver dives deep into it. His flashlight, moving in all directions, falls on a lot of junk stuck between rocky terrains under the sea. All the junk are rusted and look very dated. The diver moves into a big structure, shaped like an ice-berg, cold like an ice-berg, very fragile. Anything he touches starts perishing. He floats in, with only the limited view of a flashlight. Some more rusted junk, difficult to make out what they are. Some Iron chains are still intact in their shapes. Some earthen pots floating around and a lot of aquatic life that has built itself around it. Some wooden pieces and glasses are stuck with them and a small blurred picture trapped between those glass pieces, catches his eye. He slowly pulls it out, trying not to tear it. Photo is super blurred and no face could be made out. It looked like a man in full white clothing, a woman in pink and two children in red is what he could understand only because of the size of the blotches and some common sense. He looked hard but could not make out much. Just as he let the picture float away, something white came towards him floating slowly. A man with no diving gear is clearly breathing in water. He smiles like a human floating towards him. The diver's first instinct is to run away, but something about this man, just captivates him. His curiosity takes over his fear and he wants to know how this man could breathe underwater. He has webbed hand and feet in his built in order to aid him paddle through water easily. It was like he was born to be a resident of the sea. He swiftly floats to the diver's side and catches hold of the photo. He murmurs something and the sound vibrations create bubbles around him. The diver turns towards him, signaling him like 'who are you?' The man points at the photo and then points at his own self. Again, he murmurs something that is lost in the bubbles. But the diver could make out that maybe he is trying to say this is his photo with his family. How old is this guy, where did he come from, why is his photo in this ancient structure, is he from another century?? As he looks up to ask the next question, the man in white has disappeared. The diver moves quickly trying to find the man. He sees a white dot moving swiftly some few meters away. He follows it through, till he reaches a dark tunnel and can no more see the white dot. But he is sure the man went into this tunnel. He floats into the tunnel and suddenly feels a different energy through him. He gulps down his throat, a little frightened. Is this a good idea? Should he go further? Sounds of some mantras catch his attention. His curiosity again takes over and he floats ahead. He keeps floating and the mantras get louder as if a group of people are chanting them. There is no one in the tunnel but he can see an opening at the other end of the tunnel. He turns back to check everywhere with his flashlight, in case he missed something. His heart is beating fast and he is beginning to get tired. But he has to find out. He floats ahead to the end of the tunnel and suddenly he is in a small pond with walls on the other three sides. He looks around, trying to figure out the sound of mantras. Suddenly someone yells, 'look there is someone in the waters? Is it pishach?' The diver looks up and sees a group of people around a structure that has walls and stairs descending into this pond that he is floating in. They all gaze at him and seeing him covered in all black from head to toe, a child asks "Is he always in full black clothes papa?" Two or three men start to descend down the stairs with sticks in their hands, enough hint of the danger to the diver. He swims back into the tunnel swiftly, disappearing into darkness. All men start chanting mantras again, moving away from the structure. One man says "I think he has gone back to get more of his kind. We should immediately clear this place." Suddenly there is chaos and all men pull their children and women close, and take them away. Everybody is terrified and a guard locks the gates of the forts while all visitors leave.

Such stories and such places become perfect spots to explore. So how could I stay away from it? Me and my daredevil team of two, Aparna and Samar, came all the way to this small village of viloha in MP to explore this Devi Maa Bhavani temple that has been kept locked for many years. It is said to be haunted and under the control of Pisachas who come from under the water.

My channel on YouTube in my name "Sharman the Explorer" has been active for more than a year. I have gone to those places that have mysterious or haunted stories about it and tried to show to the audience that there is no danger. So far, we have explored four places in one year, which might seem too slow, but this is something we do on the side. We are basically engineers working in an IT company.

I was never a 9-to-5 job kind of person. Routine, discipline, restrictions, walking within the set lines bored the hell out of me. And though I was very good in Biology and many advised me to pursue a degree in medicine, I chose to go a different way with my second love, History. How did that happen? Well, that is an interesting story.

When I was young, my father would often take me to forts and I would hear the guides tell all kinds of interesting stories about these places, some too unreal, some spooky. But they left an impact on my mind and I would spend days contemplating why or how those incidents the guide was talking about, might have happened. Sometimes I would insist on going back to that place and exploring the hidden corners of the forts. I would see some writings on the walls or any peculiar thing and I would click a photograph and keep it with me. Then I would go back home and try to decode those inscriptions, but even 'The Google Baba' could not answer all my questions. I then asked my history teacher and she told me how so much of our history has been lost and we need to find them to get more information. I told her I will become a historian one day.

But like many others, who want to become pilots or musicians or model when they are young, but they ultimately end up in an engineering college because parents fear the insecurity of unconventional jobs. I understand their concern and so I obliged. Medical line would have taken more years of my life and since I was an above average student in math and science, I decided engineering would be the best option. Of course, in my head, secretly I planned to save once I got a good job and then pursue my passion for history.

Eventually, I got so used to the comforts of this corporate life and promotions and hefty salary in my account every month that being a historian would never get me. So I decided to pursue my passion for exploration as a side hobby. And here I am, gaining popularity through my channel. Now I can't wait to bust another myth by entering this temple and recording every nook and corner of it. It is such an archaeological beauty which we have abandoned because of some superstition. I might enjoy the stories of these places, but I definitely don't believe in these so-called pishachas.

We had the official permission to enter the temple but the Village Panchayat was not happy with this. They kept warning me how dangerous it is. They often hear noises from inside the temple, so definitely it's not empty. There are some negative forces in it. I argue that it's a goddess's temple, how can it have negative energy! They gave up eventually and handed us the keys to the temple. Samar is in charge of the camera that will record everything, while Aparna and I will write the content that we speak in the video. Aparna has a knack for Hindi poetry and shayari, which improves my speech and gives it a beautiful presentation.

As we try to unlock the big lock of the temple, it is rusted and required extra strength from all three of us to be able to open it. As we walk into the dark, cob-webbed temple, Samar captures every corner of this temple, its beautiful artwork on the walls and carvings that definitely told some stories. He wanted to finish everything before sunset. Aparna meanwhile entered the temple area to pray to Devi Maa and then sat on the stairs near the small pond in the center of the temple, "Sharman, this is that pond from where the pishachas come. This is what the villagers were saying." I go closer to have a look at the pond. At first it seems quite calm and boring, until I spot a small tunnel under water. I have to check it out. Samar can already see it in my eyes, "No dude! Don't even think about it!" I take out my diving gear from my bag. Of course, I brought it with me. The very theme of my channel is to break such superstitious myths that exist in our country. And what's the point of this expedition if I don't explore the tunnel and prove to the villagers that there is no pishach there when I come out safe and very much alive.

Aparna and Samar try to convince me, but my gear on me, I am ready to take the dive. I tell Samar to record me entering the tunnel and also when I come back safe. I like the tinge of nervousness I feel as it keeps me on the edge in my otherwise mundane life and routine job. As I dive into the pond, the water is chilly and my whole body goes from frozen state to numb state in a matter of minutes. Once I am well adjusted to this temperature, I take a long breath and go under water. It's a small pond and the tunnel is very near. Its pitch dark and I go back up and ask my friends for my flashlight. I finally enter the tunnel with a bright ray of light that precedes me. This definitely feels like sea water. How is that even possible?

It looks like a long tunnel ahead of me. I paddle through, exploring everything around. Some kind of rusted junk lies everywhere, could be parts of some broken ship or something. As I am lost in exploring the tunnel, I don't realize something swimming beside me, something shining in white. I turn to see a man dressed in white, looking at me with curiosity. My heart skips a beat, probably for the first time in my life. Firstly, because he could be a pishach but then he is not wearing all black like the villagers had described. Secondly, I see him wearing no diving gear and he is breathing so normally in water. Though he has webbed hands and feet but he is still so human-like. Are there humans who have gills and live underwater? Suddenly he speaks to me and all I can see is bubbles in water. What is he trying to tell me? Just then we are joined by a beautiful woman in pink. She is also like him, but really beautiful like a divine angel. But she looks worried. She tells something to the man in urgency and he points at me. They both look at me signaling me in another direction. I am totally confused and a little terrified too. But before I could go anywhere, tectonic activities start and I feel the sea bed shake. Faults and cracks are forming on it and one crack goes right between both my legs. Next thing I know, I am rising higher in the water and the crack opens into a big sea of hot lava that sends sparks everywhere. I couldn't believe my eyes. I look up and I see a group of men, women and kids, all running to a safe spot. The man who saw me first, is dragging me with him.

Suddenly it dawns on me that the tunnel was my only way back to that temple. How can I be going with them in the opposite direction? I try to resist but he is much stronger. He takes me a little further and stops. He signals me to wait, folds his hands and it looks like he is praying. Suddenly a tunnel appears right in front of us and he signals me to take this path. It takes me a few seconds to process it but as I realize, I look up and see the man swim away with his partner and kids. I wave to him and as he sees me, I fold my hands in gratitude. I dive through the tunnel and swim back into the pond. I see two villagers there, with my friends. They are chanting some mantras. I call out to Aparna and Samar. They are shocked!

Only later, I realize that I was back after almost one whole day. The concept of time underwater is very different from the land because I hardly spent an hour underwater. I sit down quietly in the car as I try to process everything that I have seen today. Something that remains hidden in the depths of the sea shall remain hidden as God intended it! Something inside me tells me I owe them my life and public knowledge of their existence is not good for them, not that anyone will believe me or I have anything that can prove my story. But one thing I have surely learnt today. No story is a myth as it stems from some event and there are lives that exist beyond the imaginations of us, land humans. And they can do such magical things that are much beyond our imagination. Suddenly I feel like I know nothing, like I am a small speck in the ocean of stardust that got saved under the blanket of humanity that protects us all!

"The realization that something exists beyond the imaginations of our limited mind, enlightens us about our mere existence."

Chapter 7

There is Always a Way

News flashes about the war situation in the North Eastern state of Manipur and a video shows two women of a certain tribe being dragged across the streets naked by the enemy clan. Of course, they have blurred the women figures, but I can feel the sudden awkwardness in the room. Papa changes the channel immediately mumbling some curse words that I choose not to listen to. From the corner of my eye, I see my brother Advik engrossed in his phone and Mamma, acting oblivious as always, starts nagging Papa, "I was telling you to put that Singing Idol show before only, at least we all could watch it together!"

Advik gets up and excuses himself, "I have to finish my homework." A melodious voice of a lady singing in high pitch, "zindagi ke safar mein guzar jaate hain jo makaam... wo phir nahi aate...." [In the journey of life, the moments that have gone... will never come back again....] I am in no mood to study or open my books even, but it's still better than listening to this. Papa has already dived into his favourite 'Newspaper'!

I am fuming from within. I look at my books, pick one and the next moment throw it away. What do men think of themselves? I feel bad for those women in the news, helplessness and pain engulfs me. I wipe my tears away. I really have to study for my math test tomorrow, but it's difficult to focus. The fear of penalty every time I get a sum wrong, even when I am just practicing in my room is overwhelming. But I also can't afford to lose marks and bear the penalty for real, where my nightmare turns into reality and scars me forever. Yeah, penalty has become a disturbing part of my life. I gulp down my emotions and go to the study room, where Advik is busy, but not doing homework. To my utter shock, I catch him watching the unedited version of the video they were showing on the news. He shuts the screen as he sees me.

"Are you sick in the mind Advik? How can you even watch this?? Go now or I will tell Mamma!" Advik wants to say something. He tries to explain himself, "It's not what you think...Actually it's..." Just then Mamma comes and looks at both of us suspiciously, "what are you guys talking about?"

Advik looks at me and is about to say something when I cover up for him, "I was just telling him to first take a shower, weekend doesn't mean no shower day." Advik shrugs his shoulder and leaves.

"Arya, instead of lecturing your brother, you should get ready; you have to go for your math tuitions." I start to perspire; "Mamma I am not feeling well, can I not go today?"

She dismisses, "you have not gone for two classes now, please get serious! You have your exams coming up."

I decide to quietly go to Lata's place instead. Never to his house! Darkness engulfs me and a hand caresses my bare shoulders. I shudder and beg, "please let me go sir, I won't make more mistakes." A man slides his hands all over me, saying, "Oh, you should, and then enjoy the penalty."

PENALTY! I mumble no, struggling to shout out a firm NO, that grows into a loud scream. There is a loud knock on my bathroom door. I come out of my trance. Mamma yells in fear, "are you OK Arya?" I am just too shaken up to say anything. I can hear Papa and Advik too, enquiring what happened. I somehow manage to reply, "I am OK mom." Tears roll down my eyes and I let the warm water wash them away. I can't show them my tears!

My father decides at the last moment to drop me for my tuition, completely ruining my escape plan. I am dying from inside. I feel like I am being taken to my executioner. The car brakes to a sudden stop. I look up; it's the signal. I spot a temple and silently say my prayers. "I am so helpless, only you can help me God!" Just then I spot a physically-challenged man with only his hands and no legs, outside the temple premises. He is picking up the shoes of devotees and placing them on the shelf nearby. When people come out after offering their prayers, he hands them their footwear and they pay him small tokens of money. That hits me hard. If this guy can fight life each day, if he is still not helpless, how can I be? By God's grace, I have two legs to walk or run on and I still can't fight this situation?! Now I think I know what to do.

That Man I call Sir, stands right in front of me, talking to Papa. No sign of shame on his face. He looks at me with such fake concern in his eyes "how are you now Arya? Hope you are all well now beta!" Beta [child]!! Do you even know the meaning of that word? Is this what you do to children?? I faintly nod, realizing Papa is looking at me. Papa leaves me behind in the hands of this monster. He closes the door and turns me towards him, his hands caressing my shoulders again. "Now what should I do with you? You should not have missed those classes!" I speak in a begging tone, "I am sorry sir, it won't happen again." He looks at me with the eyes of the executioner.

After a few minutes of misery, I had to bear to have the recording as proof about whatever he said to me, the very next instant I come up with a bathroom excuse before he tries something else. As soon as I step into the bathroom, I waste no time and jump out of the window of this jail, running as fast as possible. I am ready to expose him and his misdeeds to my parents and now it's his turn to go to jail. I reach home to tell Mamma everything, feeling pretty courageous. But the sight of her mourning on Papa's shoulder shocks me. Police is surfing through our house and I rush in to see something worse than all my nightmares, my brother Advik hanging from the ceiling fan. I go numb.

I couldn't sleep for nights. His note, his last words, saying there was no other way for him, haunt me. I wish I could tell him, "There is always a way my brother!" I have to find out what really happened. Though his classmates point out that he was absent during many classes, they have no idea why. Staff, teachers, no one knows anything! I feel so angry that no one bothered to inform me or my parents about his absence in the class. As I decide to confront the principal about this, one of Advik's juniors Nishant, who played cricket with him, corners me and tells me in a hush tone what he had witnessed. My poor brother was a victim of bullying and physical abuse by his seniors. These seniors also used to play cricket at the same ground and would often bully juniors to leave the field. After few such occurrences, my brother dared to go to their PT teacher and complain about the same. The seniors received punishments and scolding for bullying in school. They were also suspended for a week.

Out of vengeance, they started harassing Advik after coming back to school. God knows how many times he had been succumbed to their tortures. Nishant told him how Advik lived in fear but never spoke to anyone about it. Nishant tried asking him once and Advik strongly denied it saying, "don't go around saying such things. It's nothing actually. I can fight my own battles. School will unnecessarily involve parents if they get to know about this. And parents never understand these things. I will only get blamed for being rowdy."

Hearing this, took me back a few years ago when Advik had poured water on a classmate who raised his hands and hit some other classmate in the middle of a verbal fight. Advik had told us the whole story, but my parents were ashamed that they were called to school because of him. They never appreciated his courage in standing for the right! And I also remained quiet to avoid being the target of their wrath. Advik stopped sharing things at home after that. Sometimes he would share some things with me but then I grew up and I had my own set of problems that I could never share with him. We grew apart!

'Nurtured roots shape righteous fruits.' But nurturing is not only about nutrition and education, it's also about communication. Our family never discussed the real issues. Consequently, the communication gap only widened over time and our family got more and more dysfunctional. Any disturbing news or sexual topics or crime and it were just dismissed with curses and abuses, never discussed with sensitivity and maturity. So, we kids also learnt to do the same.

I could never tell my parents about the physical abuse I was going through and Advik could never tell them how he was being bullied at school. And what a heavy price we as a family, have paid for that! No point crying now! When Advik needed the right guidance from his parents, proper vigilance at school and support of his sister, he never received it. And this pushed him further into darkness. I wish I could tell my brother how I fought my darkness drawing inspiration from that physically-challenged man and swam up to the surface. Only if we had communicated, I could have helped Advik swim up to the surface! I could have saved him from drowning into the darkness. Now all I am left with is regret and pain that will stay with me forever!

Complaints will be filed, actions will be taken, evils of the society like that tutor or these seniors will face the wrath of their karma, but the life taken will never come back. Truly, "zindagi ke safar mein guzar jaate hain jo makaam...wo phir nahi aate..." My brother Advik, today is Rakshabandhan and I wish I could tie the thread of hope on your wrist and say, "There is always a way brother, there is always a way!"

"Anything strengthens when nurtured and perishes when neglected."

Chapter 8

Music knows no Boundaries!

A well-lit stage, a huge crowd shouting and cheering, a whiff of smoke that gradually spreads all over the stage, giving it a very dreamy effect. A lean and lanky figure with ruffled hair walks on to the stage in silhouette and a hand reaches for the mike. A set of lips move and a beautiful voice fills the auditorium. It's a young voice of a boy but it has so much depth and emotions in every word he utters. He sings Kishore da's "Ooo mere dil ke chaaiinn...chhaiinn aaye mere dil ko dua kijiye". The audience is totally smitten and so are the judges. He gets good scores from them and kisses the stage and walks out.

A small living room where a boy and a girl jump from their seats and rejoice, "yayyy!! I knew Satya will win today also." The girl screams in excitement while the boy gives her a hi-five, "yess Didi...now no one can stop him!!" Just then a shout from their mother makes them sit straight "Prachi, Prateek, you have exams tomorrow! Turn off the TV!!" Prachi smiles as she shuts the TV thinking, "At least I got to see Satya's performance."

Satya is greeted by his family backstage. A woman, who looks pretty high-maintenance and business-like, hugs him, "My son is such a rockstar!!! You make me so proud Satya!!" The boy hugs her back, a little teary-eyed "Mom, I am not feeling well." She replies "baby, but the press is waiting to hear from you, just another 10 minutes." Satya struggles to sit with the media. He feels he is burning up from inside. He always knew his value to his family was only because his talent got them money. Born with this talent, his mother had recognized this skill in him very early on. She pushed him into this profession from a very early age and it helped their family business too. At home, it was always about profits and numbers. Satya, who sang his songs with such emotions on stage, felt none of that in his real life. They only cropped up from somewhere within him when he sang his songs. But his life was devoid of any love. It was all about fulfilling his mother's expectations and this had become normal for him. And as far as he was bringing in the money, no one cared about the other aspects of his life.

While his mother was this cold person, his father was a drunk, depressed, irresponsible man, who escaped any work and felt no shame in enjoying the fruits of his son's labour. He would say "after all we have given birth to him, it's his duty." Satya felt his father was absent from his life. Just a man who would show up once in a while, sometimes drunk, mostly fighting with his mother but always his best self in front of the public and media, expressing his hardships in making Satya what he is today. Satya knew why his mother is so shrewd in nature, he understood everything, but he was struggling with his own mental traps. Only while singing, he felt some energy inside him that would uplift him and fill him with emotions. And when he stopped, those feelings left him, leaving him empty inside.

Prachi feels the same type of energy surge through her, while she sings a prayer song in the school assembly the next day. But when she finishes singing, she is still full of emotions, emotions for her family, her friends, her teachers, everyone who mattered or contributed to her life in some way. She wears her heart on her sleeves and whenever she listens to Satya sing, she feels he is also someone who wears his emotions on the surface, just like her. But meeting him for the first time makes her realize how different he is.

It is at his concert in her hometown Pune that they meet almost five years later. Prachi is on top of the world when she and her school are chosen to sing the chorus for Satya in his concert. She couldn't believe her luck that she would get to sing with her idol. She is rehearsing with her group everyday wanting to give her best, eagerly looking forward to their performance together.

Prachi wakes up ecstatic, on the day of the concert. First thing she prays to God "May this day go well. I wish I get to talk to Satya too." She hums the same song she heard five years back on TV while she gets ready. Choosing what to wear becomes a big task. Till today, she had never realized that she had no good clothes to wear. She digs into her cupboard and finds a red long dress that she got on her last birthday. Though not completely satisfied, she decides to make do with the best she has.

As Prachi steps into the auditorium, she is very aware of every face in the hall. Her eyes continuously gaze from one corner to another searching for that one face. He is not here yet. She joins her classmates who don't let go of this opportunity to tease her till she becomes as red as a tomato. "It feels like Valentine's Day when

I look at you." "Heyy, don't you know meeting Satya is nothing less than a Valentine's Day for her." Avni and Ridhi exchange a hi-five as they laugh teasingly. Other chorus singers have also heard them and Prachi feels super embarrassed. She shushes her friends and excuses herself. She rushes into the ladies room. She is breathing heavily. She is feeling so many things at once that she feels she will collapse. She hears some murmuring out in the corridor. She peeps out from the door and sees a group of men suited, some on phones, some clearing the way, and one lady whispering something to a boy. The boy, oh God, it's Satya. Prachi's gaze freezes as his eyes fall on her. She is very nervous and has to literally remind herself to smile. But by the time she manages a smile, he is looking elsewhere and has just crossed her, walking towards the auditorium. Prachi rushes in to see herself one more time in the mirror. His gaze is still fresh in her memory. She blushes. Ok, now it's time to go!

Prachi enters the auditorium and again he is nowhere to be seen. She assumes he must be backstage. Ridhi comes to her, "where were you? Satya was here and he waved at us, you missed it!" Now how does she tell Ridhi that he has already seen her and they have exchanged a glance. Feeling it was a little special, she smiles. Ridhi nudges her, "let's go for the practice."

Throughout the rehearsals, she is in a trance. His gaze on her flashed a million times in her head, the way he sings, his expressive face, emotions in his voice that touch her heart every time. Suddenly she feels a nudge. Her music teacher is standing in front of her looking very serious. Prachi wonders, "Oh God! What did I do now?"

"So, this is what you do in the final rehearsal?" Prachi looks terrified. She is scared that she did something wrong and they might not let her perform with Satya!

So, without knowing the reason, she starts apologizing, "I am sorry sir. Just give me one more chance." Her music teacher starts laughing "Prachi, you sang really well, especially the alaap that went into a crescendo, I want you to sing it just like that on stage, with Satya!!" Before she could speak, the Principal comes into the room and everyone wishes him in attention. The music teacher is all praise for Prachi and the Principal gives her thumbs-up while he also wishes the others. The show will start in half an hour. Prachi sneaks into the recording room and hears the last rehearsal. She couldn't believe she added her own composition to her performance and everyone liked it. What would Satya think of it?

Everyone is being given positions on stage and Prachi is now shifted to the main stage, ahead of her chorus group. Friends give her the same teasing look and everything inside her goes upside down. She just closes her eyes and in low volume, rehearses her alaap. Thinking more about what was about to happen today will not help her in any way. Prachi wants to give her best, in Satya's presence!

Audience starts to stream in and stage curtains are dropped. It becomes a little dark and Prachi keeps standing in her position, continuously rehearsing. Two three suited men come on stage, checking the mike and position on the stage. One of them shouts "lights!" stage is flooded with lots of lights flashing everywhere. It hurts Prachi's eyes, at first taking away her focus. But she adjusts to the lights and fights her way back to her practice.

Meanwhile, band starts playing the music. It's one of Satya's songs. The curtain lifts. Prachi's heartbeat is racing. Now she just wants it to happen soon as it's getting difficult to breath. Suddenly she spots her parents and her brother Prateek in the audience and waves at them. While her parents give her a thumbs up, her brother Prateek truly understands her feeling. He jumps in the same kind of excitement that her heart feels in that moment. Her fluttering heart makes her a little breathless. So, she closes her eyes and starts deep breathing. She needs to compose herself to be able to perform. And as her eyes are closed, the same voice she loves the most, falls on her ears. A smile spreads on Prachi's face as she opens her eyes and looks to her right. There, in his full glory and style, is her idol Satya, singing one of his romantic compositions "My love for you…". Its Prachi's favourite and she is smitten watching him sing live. She flows into a dreamland where it's just the two of them dancing in each other's arms moving to the beautiful beats of the song. And then she invariably joins in with her alaap, still mentally dancing to it. Her eyes are shut and her voice flows, so strong and beautiful. Everyone is smitten but she is totally unaware. As the choir intervenes, she realizes where she is. She opens her eyes and looks to her right. Satya is looking at her. He looks smitten like the others are, but Prachi wonders if she made any mistake and that is why he is looking at her like this. The positive thought that he loved her singing or he finds her beautiful, are just too good to be true.

The performance is finally over and Satya just throws a flying kiss to the audience and walks off the stage. He is again surrounded by so many suited people, who call themselves his team. Prachi wishes she could talk to him once, but intervening in his discussion with his team and talking to him in the midst of all their judgmental gazes is really unnerving. Even that lady with him, she looks very strict and reserved. Prachi is joined by her chorus group who tell her how good she was on stage. Ridhi teases her, "Satya wasn't even blinking, and he was so lost in your singing!" Prachi dismisses it, "if that was the case, he would have said something or at least smiled at me. But there was no reaction from him." Her friends tried to reason it out and a part of her wanted to believe every word they uttered. Only if all of this were true and not just wishful thinking!

Prachi's parents and her brother Prateek, along with a few aunties and uncles, congratulate her and shower her with praises. But for Prachi, in that moment, all that matters is Satya saying those things to her. As they all sit in the car, Prateek shows her the performance he recorded on his phone. Prachi watches Satya and her on two sides of the same platform and she sees this video like a million times, day dreaming. She buys an ice-cream for Prateek from her pocket money as she feels so grateful for this video. She never imagined in her wildest of dreams that this day would come and Satya will be her co-singer and she would give her best. And yes, her friends were right. He did look smitten. She just wished he had said something personally.

Meanwhile, Satya is doing an interview with some channel and he looks exhausted. Suddenly, Prachi's alaap from her performance plays in his head and he just wants to break free. Something about her music is so liberating. He excuses himself for a washroom break and for the first time ever, sneaks out from the sliding window of the washroom. He feels a little uneasy at first thinking what his mother would say. But then that alaap booms in his head and inspires him to be brave. He takes a long walk on the streets of Pune. Seeing a few people pass by, he covers his head with the hood of his sweatshirt and drops his long tresses on to his forehead, covering half his face. This would be enough to conceal his true identity.

Prachi is sitting at her balcony, doing her school work. She hears someone whistle the song she performed today, so melodiously! She looks on the streets and sees a hooded bloke walking on the other side. The hooded bloke, Satya is looking at all the apartments and the trees and everything around, while whistling the tunes, when his eyes fall on the girl in the balcony and he immediately recognizes her, the alaap girl! He waves at her, lifting his hoodie and that's when Prachi realizes it's none other than Satya. Satya! Outside her house! Prachi gets all nervous. He signals her to come down. Prachi cannot believe what is happening. The SATYA wants to meet her!

She rushes down and as she reaches her living room, her parents are watching TV. Prateek is in the adjacent room, working on the computer. Prachi tiptoes to reach Prateek and whispers in his ears. He looks all excited hearing where she is going. He asks for two minutes while he goes occupy his parents by changing channel and showing them a documentary on aquatic life at a high volume. Prachi gets the idea and she immediately sneaks out, mentally thanking her brother profusely. She rushes to the gate and as she sees Satya standing there, looking at her, it strikes her then that she is meeting him alone in person and he is going to talk to her. Her mouth gets dry and she gets a little breathless. Thankfully she had run till the gate, so her breathlessness would be seen as caused due to running while the reality is its Satya and his presence that is making her restless. Thank God he cannot see that!

Satya says Hi and Prachi manages a feeble Hi. Satya goes on about how he has not been able to get over her alaap in their performance. He is really impressed. He asks her, "Could you teach me?" Prachi just keeps looking, smiling. Satya waves at her, but she looks all dreamy. He shakes her shoulder lightly and Prachi just then hears some noise in the background. She pulls Satya in a quick impulse and pulls him to the other side of the road and starts walking quickly. Satya keeps asking what happened. But she stops only after a few meters. She apologizes, "I am sorry for being so discreet. I told no one at home that I was coming out to see you. Else they wouldn't allow me!" Satya goes like "ditto! My folks don't know either." And he raises his hand for a hi-five. She reciprocates and they laugh. Prachi loosens up a bit and extends her hand, "Hi, I am Prachi." Satya smiles, "I like your name." He shakes her hand confidently, "I loved your singing!" Prachi had to say it now, "Coming from you, it means a lot! My brother and I have watched you sing for the past five years and you are just great!" Satya moves his shoulder casually, "Naah! I am ok, you are superb. I would love it if you can teach me that alaap."

Satya and Prachi sit on a bench in a park. While Prachi breaks down her alaap, trying to teach Satya, he looks at her mesmerized!" Prachi blushes, "Hey you need to stop staring like that, it makes me nervous!" Satya laughs, "I am sorry but I am smitten by your voice. All day, it's been ringing in my ears." This feeling is so surreal for Prachi. They spend some time discussing music when suddenly Satya gets up and breaks into tap dance as he sings one of his songs. Prachi joins in, trying to match his steps. This time, he breaks it down for her so that she can get the sequence of steps. Both are lost in their creative world, unaware of some prying eyes who have already recognized Satya, dancing without his hood. Satya and Prachi move from one song to another and Prachi trips and falls trying another step. Satya bends to pick her up when he spots someone moving towards them. He freezes as he recognizes it's some people from his team. He helps Prachi get up and then they break into a run. They rush through the streets till they spot an unguarded building. Satya climbs the gates and then pulls Prachi up. They jump on to other side and run into hiding. As they stop, both are panting heavily. Prachi, trying to catch breath, is perplexed, "I understand you didn't tell anyone but why are you running like you did something wrong?" Satya laughs while panting, "You won't understand Prachi! You have a normal childhood. I am a prisoner to my fame and my family's expectations!"

They can still hear some footsteps and hide behind a bush. Suddenly some hand comes on Prachi's shoulder and she screams. They have been caught. Some man starts clicking their photos and before Satya could catch him, he runs away. His team gets there just then. They had heard Prachi scream. Satya asks them for two minutes and turns towards her, "Hey I have to go now, but I want to give you something for you to remember me by." He removes a black crystal bracelet on his wrist and gives it to her, "This is my lucky bracelet. I wear it for all my concerts. I want you to have it because your music is magical and filled with emotions that I can only recreate, but not feel. And I wish you come to Mumbai one day and become a successful singer. And this bracelet brings you luck just like it brought to me." He asks his team for his card and hands it over to Prachi, "Call me if you ever need a friend in Mumbai." Prachi is overwhelmed with emotions as she sees him walk away with his team. "I am a prisoner to my fame and family's expectations." His words ring in her ears and she realizes how his life is not as magical as she thought it was. After all, he found magic in her simple, regular life!

Next day papers become all about Satya and this new girl he was roaming with. Prachi's photo is in those papers and her parents are really mad at her. The strict lady, who now she knows is Satya's mom, just calls Prachi a crazy fan and tries to bury the news. But Satya in his next concert in Hyderabad hums her alaap and tells everyone "It's a beautiful gift to me from a special friend." Prachi wears Satya's bracelet on her wrist and looks at it. She does her singing rehearsals and recalls so many moments she got with him in one single day. The world can call it anything, but she knows how they will always be connected by music. She hides his card in her diary and writes,

"Someday again we will sing on stage together.

Our worlds won't be so different forever.

I will come to Mumbai my friend,

Where, we shall meet again!"

Chapter 9

Time Capsules for the living!

The world is turning upside down. Sea waters are filling the lands, muddy waters flowing to another bank. Mountains, not so high anymore, are sliding to even shorter heights. Cracks and faults of the earthquake shatters the mother earth to pieces. Suddenly a pile of weathered rocks roll downhill and no life is seen around. A bird perching on a rock, flutters and flies over. She scans the area as she chirps in wonder. A distant sound of choir is heard and she follows the sound. A group of about twenty human beings, all in tattered clothes, sing something that sounds like a prayer to God. While some are weeping, others are still in shock. The bird chirps, she wants to question them all, what have you done to my home? What has happened to this planet and why? Her wings flutter furiously as she flies over their heads with her squeaky chirps.

As she flutters, she sees a man face the group speaking to them, "Each of you, write five things and bury it here as a time capsule. These five points should speak to our future when this earth revives and tell the people of the future land what they must do on this planet to save it from destruction." Big cardboard pieces torn into smaller pieces paired with tin-shaped boxes, are distributed to everyone along with a pen. The man says apologetically, "this is the best we could manage in these times of extreme shortage." Some shout "don't worry, no problem" and all the People start scribbling their points one by one.

The man then asks everyone to read their chit out loud before they bury it. One woman in the first row reads with a heavy voice, "Plant more trees. Make it a compulsory rule that the number of trees you cut, you have to plant at least that much or more and if not done, it's a punishable offense." Many people nod, expressing their support in unison. Another man two rows behind her, adjusts his cap and reads, "Take care of animals and birds and use them to travel anywhere as we did in olden times, in order to avoid pollution. Also take their help to communicate through letters. Stop looking for shortcuts. Longer and more natural route is always better." An old man's shivering voice follows, "Don't make plastic and don't make factories to create any products. Use what is around you from nature, the God's creation and you will not suffer like us." An old lady next to him adds to it, "Don't destroy the mother Earth by polluting air, water, land or sky."

A young boy in front of the old lady raises his hand and screams "I have the best one!" The whole place goes quiet. The old couple behind him smiles looking at him. The young boy shouts, "I want to give this chit to God telling him not to create humans when Earth revives and there will be no problem." Everyone looks at the boy, shocked. He shrugs his shoulders, "What?! Don't be surprised! We are the most selfish ones, we think only about ourselves. Look at that bird chirping furiously, I didn't see even one of you noticing it as you are drowned in your own selfish sorrows. Why should God recreate us when we are the villains who destroyed all other lives on earth?"

Everyone is aghast while the bird goes and sits on the boy's shoulders. The innocent boy blurts loudly, "I am sorry birdie, from all my people. We destroyed your home". Another girl next to him pats the bird and says, "We knew everything that was the problem and still refused to do anything about it. Our teacher made us write in our essays about all the problems and the adults discussed all that among themselves, but never did anyone work on the actual solutions. What a sad world we live in." The young boy pats the bird with a frown on his face. Some other kids join too and they apologize to the bird and then to God, "Sorry Almighty!" they say in unison.

But God spares them all and they live on. They build the world again from whatever was spared. Growth leads to necessity and necessity to more inventions in the name of development. When days become better, people get back to their old ways, servants to their own selfish habits. World destruction begins again, like before.

When natural disaster strikes, floods bring water to the homes and livelihoods are destroyed. Some time capsules that were buried years back, come floating by and a man walking with his son, picks one of them. His young son had spotted this tin box and the man could recall what it would contain. He opens the tin box and out comes a crushed cardboard piece that he straightens out with his hand. He is reminded of that day when he had written those five points when the world, they believed to be their home was about to end. And how life moves in full circle, made him laugh. But his laugh fades away after what he reads on the chit. His son comes to him and says "papa i found another one" and he reads it "I want to give this chit to God telling him not to create humans when Earth revives and there will be no problem."

The man's eyes tear up as he hears those very words he wrote as an innocent child, wise words forgotten in the course of life. Just then he spots a bird chirping furiously at his window. He tells his son "I wrote this son". His son looks at him, surprised, while his father continues, almost resonating the same thoughts, " what?! Don't be surprised! We are the most selfish ones, we think only about ourselves. Look at that bird chirping furiously, we have destroyed her home too. Why should God recreate us when we are the villains who destroyed all other lives on earth?" His son looks at the bird, blinking innocently "I am sorry birdie, from all my people. We destroyed your home." The man hugs his son and says, " no son, I am sorry, I knew everything that is the problem and refused to do anything about it. We read about these problems, wrote in our speeches but never worked on the actual solutions. What a sad world we live in. I am sorry for creating this sad world for you, please forgive me son! I repeated the mistakes my ancestors made." The man weeps his heart out while his son looks at the bird, concerned as she flutters her wings furiously, against the glass of a window. Every knock of her fluttering wings feels like a question she demands an answer to. But the man couldn't look into her eyes out of utter shame. The bird finally gives up as she gets no answer and flies away. Like poor mother Earth, she also has finally given up on humans!

"When we don't work in sync with the nature, when we don't protect our home, when we don't value what we have, it gets taken away."

Chapter 10

Under-Construction

A football is being kicked around on a muddy playground. The ball rolls from one foot to another really fast. Some cheering and shouting can be heard as two pair of feet take over the ball and pass it among themselves in the same direction. More feet follow their path trying to catch up. The ground has made all their shoes dirty and soaked in mud. One of the two, leading the pack, kicks the ball hard and a struggling pair of feet fall to the ground as the ball hits the goal. There is some jumping and cheering and a bunch of kids huddle together and shout "hip hip hooray!" while some kids call their team mates and discuss secretly, that too huddled together. I, with my red shoes tell my team to buckle up. We are falling behind. I change position of players and throw thumbs up in the air. Game begins again. A cute chubby girl sitting on a bench on one side writes 1-0 with a chalk on her slate.

Ball is in my control, but I see lot of shoes blocking my way. I pass it to a black shoe on my right as I clearly know its Atul, my teammate. But somehow, he fails to take over and the ball falls in the hands of the enemies. Ball is again moving in the opposite direction and I have to stop it somehow. I splash through a muddy puddle and manage to reach in a blocking position. Yes, ball is just a few inches away. I take an adventurous dive and they lose the ball. Taking position, I kick the ball with all the energy in the opposite direction aiming for it to get closer to the goal. But the ball collides with a small rock and changes direction. It rolls in the direction away from the field through a small pathway into a big building under-construction.

Everyone groans. My teammate yells, "What have you done Nakku?! Now who will step into that haunted building to get the ball?" Everyone looks at me, "Actually we all can go together, and then we won't be afraid." Everyone refuses. Everyone is terrified of that building. All this began when one day we all were playing on the terrace on my birthday and it had gotten a little late. From the back side of my house, that under-construction building was visible. The building has been like that for so many years now. Few years back, workers would come; construction would go on everyday till the skeleton of the building was erected. Then suddenly work stopped and no one came to that building. And it's been like that for so many years. We always wondered why the building was so isolated.

So that night, my friend Arvind got this crazy idea to play a game where we guess why this building has been abandoned. He started the story about how it must be haunted and the ghosts scared the workers away. We all got a little spooked and I got up to switch on more lights on the terrace, when I spotted some light flashing in that dark isolated building. I rushed to my friends and drew their attention to this. All of us got really scared as the light flashed through the windows of the building, like someone was walking inside. And it was so late at night that we all assumed it must be some ghost or as my friend Aviral pointed out, it could be some kidnapper's hiding point. He loved his mystery novel stories and always filled our head with all this crap. Now every time we would go to the playground, we would stay away from that building at any cost.

Almost 6 months back, Atul had once by mistake, kicked the ball into that building, but he was so scared to go there that he had to buy a new ball for us. He got scolding at home but he preferred that to entering this supposedly haunted place. My problem was I will get scolded at home and on top of that my parents will try to reason with me that my fear is unreasonable and might even force me to go to the building and get the ball. So, I might as well go now only! I knew I had no choice in this matter but to enter this haunted building and bring back the ball. Atul insists it's better to get another ball but I decide I have to give this a try. Aviral hands me a stone and asks me to throw it at the ghost and run. I keep the stone in my pant pocket and take a few deep breaths. I finally reach the entrance of this under-construction building and stop.

I look up to see a huge building that looks like a haveli with arched big windows that one sees in those old Rajasthani palaces. It already looks so dark, isolated and dated from outside and the dim light of the dusk with no sunlight only makes it spookier. I believe the ball hasn't gone that far and all I have to do is run into the hall, pick up the ball and run out as fast as I could. I am preparing my mind and body for this. I want to do it like ripping a bandage, swiftness will make it painless. I take two steps towards it and turn back to see all my friends standing a few feet away. Everyone is terrified.

Near the entrance of this building, there are mini hills of sand and bricks. There are broken buckets and cement marks on the wet ground. As I am busy observing them, one of the buckets falls down and something wiggles past it. I feel chills pass through me. Atul yells, "Nakku it must be a snake, be careful!" I am terrified of any reptile and snakes are the worst. I move a few steps back. Invisible ghosts and now live animals, its only getting worse and scarier! Just then I spot a black cat with green eyes staring at me directly and meowing. I stare back, terrified. Then it settles down, purrs and curls up on the wet ground near the entrance. It must be the cat that toppled the bucket. Stupid Atul! He scared me more with a snake.

It's very dark inside the haveli as I take a step in through the entrance. In the dim light of the evening streaming in, I spot a switchboard next to the door I entered from and I switch on a bulb hanging from the ceiling. The switchboard has a layer of dust on it. Bulb light streams into the room well and my eyes are scanning the floor for our ball. Sound of birds fluttering away and I duck automatically as a reflex action. I look around and there is no sign of the ball. I wonder how hard I kicked it that it rolled far into this building. I walk a little further towards the stairs hoping the ball would have rolled to the area under it. I spot a few clothes hung here and there over the windows and some abandoned machineries lying on the floor. I bend down to touch one when I feel a sting on my feet. Aah! I look down and I am standing over a queue of ants. Some have climbed on to my feet and I stamp my feet hard to drive them away. I also swiftly move forward towards the stairs. As I approach the area under the staircase which is very dark, I spot something white. I think I have found our ball. I bend to adjust to the height of the area and move forward. Just when I reach that white object, I hear a loud thud on the staircase above me!

I am terrified. My hands are shivering. Somehow, I manage to pick up that white object that thankfully is the ball I was looking for. I can hear my friends calling out to me, worried that I am not out yet. Feeling the ball in my hand, I start to rush out to leave this building, never to return again. But I hear another thud and I freeze. I peep from the edge of the staircase and see a room above and I see some shadows move into that room. Someone is up there. I can see the entrance door on the other side, directly in my view. All I need to do is not stop for anything and storm out. I keep checking for the shadows that moved into the room, hoping they won't come out.

As I take a few steps out of the dark area under the staircase and move into some light, I spot a shadow come out of the room. I yell and run for my life as I see the shadow from the corner of my eye, rush towards the stairs, wanting to come down to me. I run like I have never run before, my heart pulsing so fast that I feel like it's going to stop beating.

Out through the entrance door, I topple over the hill of sand and fall. Everything blurs in sight and I have come at such high speed that I am unable to stop. I somersault into a pool of mud. The ball rolls out of my hand. My friends call out to me from a distance. And behind me, I can hear dogs barking and it's only getting louder. Are they approaching me? I look up and wipe the mud off my face, ready to break into a run, when I see that my friends are not calling out to me. They are running and shouting for their lives as dogs are chasing them on the playground. I have bruises and scratches on my elbows and knees, they might even be bleeding a bit, but another barking sound behind me and I break into a run blindly. No time to feel pain and cry over it when a dog is so close to you, chasing you all through the ground. I am running as fast as my feet could carry me. I see Aviral with a dog running so close to him and I look behind to check only to find this dog behind me, closing in too. Running on a muddy ground, splashing over puddles and 'aahing' in pain once in a while, all this kept going on for some time. The dogs are not giving up!

I spot a house on my right as I am running and I immediately turn towards the right. I need to reach this house and ask for help. But first, I climb the car parked right in front of the house. Two dogs come near the car and they start barking, jumping hard, and trying to reach me. I somehow need to reach the door of this house, but even extending my hand could be dangerous. Suddenly I remember the stone that Aviral gave me before entering the building. I take it out of my pocket and throw it hard towards the door. A man comes to the door with a stick and chases the dogs away. By then, my friends have also joined me there who stand near this man. The dogs fear the stick in his hand and they have no choice but to back down. They go away.

We thank the kind uncle and come back to the ground. It's dark now! Time to go back home! We are all shaken up with this experience and no one says anything. Just then the white muddy ball comes flying at us and we see it was from the small passage near the under-construction building. We quietly pick the ball and leave the playground. No one is curious; No one wants to know anymore. I don't know about the invisible ghosts or kidnappers, but the live animals like dogs have scared us enough for a day!

"Under-construction minds of the young have vast imaginations that can easily be under illusion."

Chapter 11

Time machine

I open the door into a dark room. The floor creaks as I move down the stairs. I pull on a string and suddenly a bulb lights up, revealing a dark foggy room with only this dim bulb light illuminating it. There is a lot of junk and cartons kept in the room. There is a book shelf in one corner which mostly has Archaeological books. There is sound of machinery in the background. My eyes immediately close on to a book that is kept in the middle of the row of books. The title reads "Her Last Expedition" on the spine of the book. There is a thick layer of dust and I cough as I shuffle through these books, dusting them a little. I pull out that book and place it on a wooden table on my right. I open the first page of the book. It has a picture of a lady and below her picture, her name Heidi Jones and dated 1785 - 1815. On the Adjacent side, it's written

"An early death due to an unfortunate mishap on her last archaeological expedition into the dark and mysterious caves of Kanika." Below this in bigger font, it's written in capitals, "MANY HAVE TRIED TO EXPLORE THE MYSTERIES OF THIS HIDDEN CAVE, BUT NEVER CAME BACK TO TELL THE STORY. IS THE CAVE HAUNTED??" I momentarily pause on the word HAUNTED. I look around the room and feel lonelier and a little scared too. Just then, I notice a phone booth like structure and I move closer to explore it. It has a crooked door with some green vegetation that has developed on it. The door opens and instantly an audio begins. It's a woman speaking in a machine-like voice "Hello. Please start the time machine after the instructions. Please listen to the instructions carefully to avoid any mishap. This machine will take you to your desired time zone once you hit the level and the start button but kindly listen carefully to this warning message, remember that you need to enter this cabin within 15 minutes into that time zone, else there is no return and this machine will retrace its steps to its original position. Have a safe ride." There is some whirring sound of the machine. I sigh and blow out air to release the tension. I see buttons on one side of the cabin. The first button reads location. On pressing that, the same woman's mechanical voice is heard this time saying "your location please". I stammer, "Kanika Caves". Next my finger clicks on Time. Woman asks "what time and day sir?" He replies "7:45 PM October 10, 1815." Woman says again "your ride is ready to take off sir. Please click on the start button to begin your ride." My fingers move towards the start button, a little shaky and hesitant. The machine sound is whizzing smoke and it's grown even louder. The woman's voice asks again "Do you need more time sir?" I exclaim, "No no, I have waited long enough. I need to unveil this mystery in order to sleep peacefully." Determined, he clicks on the start button, not hesitating anymore. The cabin door disappears from sight and everything goes into a whirlpool of smoke and dust.

Caves in darkness all around and not a single source of light, I immediately take out a flashlight in my pocket and turn it on. I move its beam everywhere, exploring the area. I breathe heavily as I feel there is not enough oxygen. Just then I hear multiple footsteps approaching. I lower my beam and find a corner to hide. Who are these people? I look on, waiting in total defensive mode. Could it be ghosts as the book had mentioned. Suddenly, multiple beams of torch light spread through the dark caves revealing the contours of the caves. One of those beams move from one side of the cave to the other, exploring every corner. Four footsteps are heard walking ahead following the beam of light. A woman's voice is heard talking to herself saying in between her panting "My students would have loved to see this, but I couldn't put their life in danger." The torch beam goes a little further and splits into two corridors. A map is held up at the eye level and the same woman reads, her fingers tracing the pathways as she reads "Right corridor goes to an orchard, while the left corridor...ummm...yeah, it goes to this closed cabin." There is a cross marked at that spot on the map. I am far behind her, so I can only see her head and the map she is holding up. Who is she? And there are three other men right behind her, following her instructions. Suddenly, she exclaims "So after roaming for so long, I am very close to my destination." The footsteps fasten as they move to the left side and start exploring further. It's a straight corridor and after a brisk walk of about two minutes, they see a small wooden door ahead. They rush towards it panting excitedly. The woman's hand tries to push the door open, but it does not budge. There is some scraping sound on my right and I see a rat as the torch light hits it and it runs away. Some loud thud sounds and the men have managed to break the door, unlocking to reveal the shimmer and sparkle inside that could be seen even through that small door and as they entered, revealing a room which has so much treasure and every object there is made of gold, the woman exclaims "Oh MY God!! This is breath taking. So, this is what has been hidden for so long in these dark trenches." They had not gone far inside, when a loud thud is heard outside the room. I scan the opposite side, towards the door. No sign of anyone. Suddenly the woman yells and runs out of the small door followed by the other men, screaming for their lives. My torch follows through to reveal a big boulder coming towards them. They break into a run back through the dark corridor with the torch beam light dancing in all directions. They can hear many footsteps behind them and someone yelling in a heavy voice "Catch them now and bring them Alive!!! Hahahaha!!!!" Their footsteps accelerate and so does the footsteps of the lady. They reach the juncture where they turned left and instead of running straight, they take a right." One of the men check the time; its 7:53 PM. The man's voice exclaims "Just 7 minutes. Oh shit!!!!" He still runs alongside the woman till they reach an orchard. I follow them through, from a distance. They run across the orchard, cross a bridge and run up the stairs. After two to three flights, there is one small cabin. They enter it feeling safe. Of course, the boulder cannot go up the stairs. I turn back to check where it is, but it's nowhere. The lady runs her fingers through the map. Suddenly I realize I am not tracking my time. I check and my watch is showing 7:55 PM. "Oh no!" I panic nervously. The door opens and I rush back through the same dark corridors when I hear a loud bang sound. I turn to see the staircase and the whole cabin burst into flames. Shocked and in panic, I retreat a few steps back. Suddenly the floors start shaking and the noises of structure falling behind, ground making loud noises of destruction falls in my ears. But I can't turn back anymore. I am feeling like any moment, ground will collapse from under my feet. Suddenly my watch alarm starts beeping suddenly and I realize it's 7:59 PM already. I keep running but something feels weird. I look down to see my feet's retreating back as something is pulling me behind, into a big dark hole. I am trying to scream but all I could get out was a squeaky noise amidst my panting for breath. And suddenly everything goes dark.

All that darkness I was falling into, takes me deeper and deeper down the hole till I feel something under me. I try to get up, struggling to locate my time machine, but it is nowhere to be found. I am running out of time. It will leave me and go. But I am not able to move. I want to scream but nothing comes out of my mouth. My hands, my body, my head, my neck, even my legs, everything is paralyzed. My alarm is still ringing in my ears and my eyes are struggling to see where I am. I fear for my life, I think I am going to die soon. And no one will know as I am in a different era. Tears stream down my eyes as I remember my family, my parents, my sister and my friends. I keep trying to get up, in the hope that I can save myself somehow. I am never gonna see them again. As I squeeze my eyes to clear my vision of all the tears, I see a mirror near my feet and I see me running to come out of it but I am falling behind, into a big hole behind me. I can only mouth help as the helplessness is killing me!

I see reflection of a tube light in the mirror that storms my eyes with its intensity. I blink my eyes twice as I adjust to the light around. I am breathless and the alarm is still ringing. I look around the room. I can move my neck again. I turn immediately, feeling my bed is completely drenched in my sweat. I take two minutes to make sense of what just happened. I have read about sleep paralysis, but I experienced it for the first time. And it didn't feel any less than being in a horror story. I move every part of my body and I am not paralyzed anymore thankfully.

I get up and sit, breathing deeply to calm down. Drinking some water helps my nerves. I come out of my trance and realize I am on a bed, but it's in my study, a small room with the same book shelf as I had seen in the basement. I shut the annoying alarm. Its 4:30 in the morning. I feel something under my other hand and it's the same book with the woman's photo and the same content about Heidi. There are sweat stains on the page and it's a little crushed too. I straighten out the page and close the book. Its cover reads "Her last Expedition".

I wash my face. I am still trying to process that feeling. The dream felt so real as if the story of the book has become my present reality. But definitely my imagination was much worse that the actual reality, or is it? Well, only time will tell as I will read on, eventually. For now, I go into my balcony, sit on my yoga mat and breathe deeply.

"Our imaginations stem from the books we read and they seep into our dreams and reality."

Chapter 12

The Convicted father

A middle-aged father is waking up his daughter Aadira. Her bed is covered with her school books on one side. She lifts her fingers signaling two more minutes. He smiles thinking she stayed up late last night, studying. He stacks her books neatly and keeps them on her study table. He plants a kiss on her forehead and walks out of the room.

His younger daughter Amara is ready for school. He ties her hair into a knot while she is notoriously pulling her hair out. They keep laughing as the father tickles her till she gives up. A woman yells from the other room to stop playing and hurry up! The man's face gets serious as he holds his finger to his lips and signals his daughter by pointing at the watch that they are getting late. She laughs quietly, her cute chubby fingers pressed against her lips too as she obeys her father and gets up to leave. Father hands her the water bottle and pins a handkerchief to her uniform. He puts the bag on her shoulders, holds her hand and rushes out.

Two girls Aadira and Amara rush out of the house as their father follows them with tiffin and bottles in his hands. The bus is waiting in the background. As they reach near the bus, their father kneels on his knees as they both plant a kiss on his cheeks, take their tiffin and bottles and immediately board the bus. As the bus goes, his daughters wave at him from the rear glass and he keeps waving back until they are out of sight. Then he walks back towards the house and opens the door.

It's a different house. He looks around, calls his wife "Meghna! Meghna!" as he walks through every empty room of the house. The same man who was laughing with his daughters, now looks lost and helpless. His eyes are puffed and he has dark circles around his eyes indicating he has not slept all night. He sits on the sofa, sipping coffee and thinking to himself. There is lot of tension on his face and he is deep in thought. Just then his phone rings bringing him out of his trance and interrupting his thoughts. He picks it up, says hello, but gets no reply. He cuts the call and keeps the phone on the table. His eyes fall on the file right next to it and he picks it up. He slowly opens it to find a bunch of papers in it. He reads through each paper carefully. Each paper is a notice from police station regarding different cases that his wife has put on him. He has been convicted for dowry, harassment, cruelty and mental abuse in the past 14 years of his marriage. He then comes across the separation papers dated a year back. And finally, a bunch of lawyer bills. He closes the file and holds his head tightly in grave tension. He reaches for the phone and calls the next number on his dial list, Lawyer Swapan. He gets a voice message saying, "please leave a message when it beeps". He says "call back" and cuts the call. He keeps the phone down, picks his towel and goes to take bath, comes out, checks his phone, does his puja by chanting some mantras, trying hard to focus. He again tries calling his lawyer, but no response.

The man is dressed in shirt and denims, combed his wet hair back neatly. He is ready and exits the house, locks the door, sits in a metro. As he is walking towards the studio where he works, he stops at a road side eatery to have dosa, his face still in tension, totally lost somewhere. Two poor kids pass by, begging on streets. As he notices them, he leaves his breakfast, buys two packets of biscuits and gives it to them. They become very happy and seeing them smile brings a grin on his face, instantly reminding him of his daughters' faces smiling at him as they walk away hand-in-hand, up till some distance, turn around waving and smiling back at him. The man struggles to hold back his tears, wondering how they are and where they are staying!

He enters the editing studio and sits at his system. He opens up the episodes which he needs to finalize that day. His assistants inform him, "Sir, the creative of their show wants to come and see the final edit. She was asking when?" He nods, signals them to wait and then checks his phone again. Still no call, he is not able to focus at work, he gets up and leaves the room.

He calls his best friend Madhav and expresses his situations and his desire to meet his kids, "It has been almost a year now since Meghna left with our kids. And she never tells me where they are. She does not allow me to meet them. I love my girls so much and I miss them every day." Madhav tells him over the phone, "Avinash! Focus on your career and clearing your name of all the false charges that have been filed against you. Only then can you try for custody or even hope to see your daughters." Avinash's suppressed frustration finally pours in his troubled voice, "But the lawyer is not doing anything about it and Meghna, the woman I loved with all my heart, how she could falsely accuse me like this. Have I ever asked for dowry or hit her in our 14 years of marriage? I understand she doesn't want to live with me, but why she is being vengeful! I will leave her alone to live her life the way she wants to or with whoever she wants to but so should she...And my kids, they are my life...and she doesn't even allow me to meet them. I very well know they want to meet me, they miss me, I was like their best buddy, and now it's been so long since I have seen them or heard their voice...I really miss them yaar.." The friend tells him that these things take time and he has to be patient. It's clear from the friend's tone that he is fed up of these complaints, after he has heard them so many times in the past one year. This is true with all his other relatives as well who have started ignoring calls from him because he keeps defending and justifying himself in the current situation. His friend Madhav still tries to keep his cool and offers to get him in touch with some other lawyer who can handle his case better, "you just take care of the money bro!" Avinash continues to sound hopeless, "no lawyer can do anything now, they are all just having fun out of my misery.." Madhav excuses himself saying someone is at his door and cuts the call. Of course, Avinash knows by now, he has cried too much to the point of driving his friends and family away. His sister's words ring in his ears, "Forget about your past...your kids are gone, they will forget you, you need to move on!"

He finishes his editing, calls up the creative and is briefing her on the edit. Just then he gets a call from his lawyer. He hands the other call to his assistant and rushes out with his phone. He is infuriated and fires him with questions, "Where have you been all day? How can you not care? My life is totally ruined and you are minting money out of my misery!" The lawyer tries to calm him down but with no convincing or positive answer, Avinash gets little frustrated, "Avinash, I was trying to sort out a deal for you in exchange for them taking back all these false charges...Just give me time.." Avinash cuts him mid-sentence, "I just want to know when can I meet my children."

He is lunching with his team, people around him do not know about his condition. They are busy with their regular chit-chats. He is just gulping down his food to fill his tummy. He has not enjoyed his meals for ages now. Are his kids getting good food? Meghna hardly ever cooked!

We see him in the corner of the cafeteria, away from the crowd, speaking to someone, "Yes sir, I will come see you soon, don't you worry. In ten days, I will return the full amount." Avinash is really worried, "Sir...I know it's been 6 months...but please understand..." the call is cut on the other side followed by the loud beep sounds.

Avinash joins his colleagues, still deep in thoughts...His fellow editor Nithin cracks a joke about marriage and wives and Avinash neither hears it nor laughs, while all the others at the table go crazy with laughter. One of his colleagues jokingly say "Look at Avinash, marriage has made him so serious!" Avinash forces a smile on his face.

He walks through the beach watching families having fun together...Eating vadapav and watching kids play on the street...He distributes chocolates and tries to get some happiness seeing their happy faces. He meets moneylender at an office and hands him over a cheque...His bank balance displayed on his mobile screen is very low. He feels even more lost! He is walking back home. He checks the time, its 4, he takes a rickshaw and goes to Hare Krishna temple ISKON. He chants, listens to kirtana, and he sits there for a while seeking some peace of mind. His eyes get moist looking at the deity. He prays for his children. He walks back home, its quiet a long distance to home. While walking back he sees family in the car, small kids with their dad on bike, all these things make him miss his kids more! He reaches home, mentally and physically exhausted.... His phone rings, he sees the call, the call is from a friend Bharat and he owes him some money too. He does not pick up. He gets a message. He reads the angry messages from him warning him sternly, "Dude I need my money back. I have loans to pay for my car, you better return my money soon!" He lies down on his bed, goes through the pictures from his phone gallery. There are pictures of him and his kids on his shoulders, He and his kids at the beach, Them at the pool. He sees Meghna in that picture., zooms on her, "Why Meghna, why you ruined everything that was good between us?"

Meghna is yelling at him "It's been two months since we have not received any income. How will we survive without money? I am just fed up now!" He retorts back, "I am trying my level best Meghna but things are little difficult professionally. I also want to get out of this crisis soon and give a better life to our kids, you think it's easy for me to deal with all this?" Meghna turns to the other side, furiously folding dry clothes on the bed. Avinash calms down and goes to his wife and hugs her saying "All I need is your support...I will get us out of this soon!"

Avinash opens his Gmail on the laptop and drafts a mail to the commissioner of police and to the police thane where the case has been registered at Indore, seeking help for access to his children. He mails them to his lawyers too. Indore is where Meghna's parents stay!

We show him getting up in a hurry. He checks the time. Its 4 in the morning, he gets fresh and starts chanting. His mind is everywhere except in chanting. Still he keeps trying. Some where he feels, God can do some miracle and make it all like before. He cannot give up hope! He starts crying, His guilt takes over as he knows some where he is also at fault for this position in his life today, but now he wants a chance to rectify and build a good future for his kids.

After years of court battle, Meghna could successfully prove he was guilty. A loan that Avinash took from her rich father, to pay the school fees of his daughters, was shown as dowry and of course a few more planted evidences put him in jail. He lost the custody of his children forever.

After 7 years, he is out of jail. The court had ordered him to stay away from his kids. First thing, he goes to his lawyer to challenge this decision. But what he sees there, shocks him. Meghna's father and her lawyer are sitting with his lawyer, giving him some envelope. Avinash was not wrong. His intuition always told him his lawyer was bribed and has sold his soul to his wife's father. A tear or two roils down his cheek, no one will fight my case and I will never meet my kids!

He is more frustrated now. He enters his house with some groceries. He is preparing food and his actions are very rough. He is on call simultaneously and is abusing his assistant for not doing his work properly. In the background, TV is playing the old videos of his children while he is chopping vegetables. He cuts his hand with the knife, puts his hand immediately under water while he looks at the TV with a longing look. He begins to weep profusely.

He is outside a school; standing near a car and looking at kids come out of school. This is where his private investigator had told him, he would find his kids. He is checking around for any signs of security to gauge how closely he can see his children. It has been so many years. Will they acknowledge him?

Just then, he spots Aadira followed by Amara strolling out of the school gates. He tries to catch their eye by rolling a ball on the ground towards them. It lands right in front of the Aadira's feet. She gets down to pick it up and turns in his direction to check who it belongs to. She looks at him eye to eye, followed by the Amara. The younger daughter starts to move in his direction, but the elder one stops her and they immediately turn and walk away swiftly leaving him completely shocked. He suddenly drops on the floor, heart-broken, holding his head in pain and tears and frustration. He is not able to believe that his kids also don't want to meet him. He starts to hit his head hard and cry out loudly in pain. Many people start to gather. He continues to hit his head as a few struggle to stop him from further hitting his bleeding head.

In a hospital, Avinash is sprawled across the floor holding a photo of him, his wife and kids to his chest and talking to himself just like talking to his daughters, "Aadira, Amara, remember me, your dada!" He is constantly calling out their names, "Have some Poha na, I know you love it. Why are you both not eating? Don't you love your dada anymore?" He looks around, "hey let me get my car. I will take you to the beach and we will have ice-cream, what say girls? Amara, no pulling your hair, I made it this morning. See Aadira, she is such a good girl. She finished her homework. Now it's your turn! Be a good girl, come sit, sit na!" then he tries to listen but there is no one. Only he hears voices as though they are talking to him and laughs at the imaginary jokes. Nurses come and put him on the bed as he keeps laughing, "My daughters are hilarious!" He is injected with medicines that immediately put him to sleep.

Many men go through this trauma as the law favours empowering women and suppressed sections of the society. But some women wrongly use the law to fulfill their demands. So, while women have their own set of traumas to deal with, men are not far behind in that department!

"A loving father can get convicted for being a bad husband. He might have failed as a husband, but as a consequence, his fatherhood suffers."

****

9 789348 543745

Printed at Repro India Ltd.